GUNSLINGER BREED

Gunslinger Clint Halloran rides into Plainsville to help his pal Jeff Deacon, hoping to end his friend's troubles. But Deacon is on the point of being lynched, so he fires a shot. Now Halloran has a fight on his hands, a situation complicated by the crooked deputy sheriff, Dan Ramsey, who has his own agenda. Halloran, refusing to give up the fight, vows to keep his gun by his side — right until the final shot is fired.

CORBA SUNMAN

GUNSLINGER BREED

Complete and Unabridged

LINFORD
Leicester

First published in Great Britain in 2010 by
Robert Hale Limited
London

First Linford Edition
published 2012
by arrangement with
Robert Hale Limited
London

British Library CIP Data

Sunman, Corba.
    Gunslinger breed.- -(Linford western library)
    1. Western stories.
    2. Large type books.
    I. Title II. Series
    823.9'2–dc23

    ISBN 978–1–4448–1061–5

Published by
F. A. Thorpe (Publishing)
Anstey, Leicestershire

Set by Words & Graphics Ltd.
Anstey, Leicestershire
Printed and bound in Great Britain by
T. J. International Ltd., Padstow, Cornwall

This book is printed on acid-free paper

1

Clint Halloran spurred his sorrel to the crest of a rise and gazed down the reverse slope. An orange glare in the night sky had been attracting his attention for the last couple of miles and he had hoped to set eyes on Plainsville ever since he reached the high and wide prairie on his long ride north to Kansas. He sighed with relief as he took his first look at the single street below, although there was little to see beyond the splashes of lantern light emanating from the straggling buildings of the community, but the thought of hot food and a glass of beer eased the ache of long travel filling his powerful body.

He stepped down from the saddle to stretch his travel-cramped legs and flex his muscles. So this was Plainsville, he thought. He had heard enough about the place from his saddle pard, Jeff Deacon. Jeff had left him in Indian Territory a month earlier to return to Plainsville in response to a letter from his father, Asa, informing him of trouble looming. Halloran would have ridden with Deacon, but a gun contract had prevented him from accompanying his saddle pard.

He was hoping he was not too late to support the Deacon family, who owned the Big D cattle ranch in Sunset Valley ten miles west of Plainsville. He glanced around into the shadows, using his ears as well as his eyes to check his surroundings for trouble; a habit formed from ten years of gun-slinging across the length and breadth of the West. He and Jeff Deacon had made an unbeatable pair during their travels, their gun prowess earning them a good living.

Halloran swung back into the saddle and touched spurs to the flanks of the sorrel. The animal, sensing a stall and feed waiting in the town, lunged

2

forward eagerly, and Halloran curbed it with a firm hand. His big figure — he was two inches over six feet in height and weighed a lean two hundred pounds — was powerful, formidable, and there were few men who fancied their chances when they stood toe to toe with him. He was dressed in a broadcloth suit and wore a Colt .45 in a tied down holster on his right hip. His black Stetson was pulled low over his keen blue eyes, and the taut expression on his angular face gave early warning of peril to any who cared to read the signs of his appearance.

His hard white teeth gleamed as he smiled at the thought of meeting up with Jeff again. The silence of the night pressed in around him, broken only by the steady beat of the sorrel's hoofs. He rode with his reins held in his left hand while his deadly right hand rested on his right thigh close to the butt of his low-slung gun. His head turned from side to side as he looked around for signs of trouble, which was never far away, and he was ready to slip into action like a well greased spring.

The surrounding shadows were dense, almost impenetrable despite the thin crescent moon showing above a distant peak, and the pale shine from the countless stars sprinkled across the wide, illimitable sky projected a patchwork of deceptive shadows across the range. The breeze blowing in his face carried the scents it had collected during its incessant wandering from the Rockies, and he breathed deeply of its clean, heady fragrance.

He entered the town at a canter and rode along its length, his keen gaze noting the lay-out for future reference. Oil lamps were burning at regular intervals along the street, throwing pools of yellow light across the sidewalks. He saw a number of saloons with signs of their trade stuck on dusty windows. Most were almost silent, but he glimpsed figures inside. However the largest saloon was more brightly lit and far noisier. Someone was thumping a strident piano with more effort than

4

skill, and laughter and loud voices hurled echoes across the darkened street.

Halloran reached the end of the street and turned the sorrel to ride back to the big saloon. He needed a drink before stabling the sorrel, and after taking care of the animal he would get a slap-up meal — beef steak with all the trimmings. He tied his horse to a hitch rail where three mounts were standing patiently and, as he stepped on to the boardwalk the batwings of the saloon were thrust open and several men emerged in a rush. Two of them were holding a struggling man who was trying ineffectually to break their hold. Lamplight shone on the victim's face, and Halloran was shocked when he recognized his longtime pard Jeff Deacon.

A third man, behind the two holding Deacon, clutched a pistol in his right hand and was waving it in high excitement. Halloran sidestepped the group as they lunged across the sidewalk. He palmed his .45 and slammed the long barrel against the head of the nearest man holding his pard. Deacon broke free from the second man and whirled to face the man at his back. Halloran saw the third man levelling his pistol at Deacon, and triggered his gun instantly.

The crash of the shot hammered through the silence like a thunderclap. The slug smacked into the chest of the man with the gun and he screeched like a stuck pig as he went down in a heap, his gun falling from his hand. Deacon pivoted back to face the man who had been holding him, and swung his left fist in a tight arc which delivered his bunched knuckles against the man's jaw. Halloran pointed his gun at the men now thrusting through the batwings to get a view of the grim proceedings, and all movement ceased.

Deacon drew his gun and the men at the entrance to the saloon turned like a herd of stampeding steers and retreated into the building, leaving the batwings swinging. Deacon turned to face Halloran. His assailants were lying on the boardwalk between them.

'Say, thank you, mister, for stepping in against those polecats,' Deacon said, and then caught a glimpse of Halloran's face in the yellow lamp light emanating from the saloon. 'Clint! Hey, man, I'm sure glad to see you! Those galoots were fixing to string me up to the nearest tree. You sure turned up at the right moment, pard.' He held out his right hand and Halloran grasped it.

'You look like you're up to your neck in trouble,' Halloran observed. He bent over the wounded man, saw a splotch of blood high on the chest, and straightened. 'He'll need a couple of weeks in bed,' he observed. 'So what is this ruckus about, Jeff?'

'These three are a part of the trouble I came home to. The guy you shot is Rufus Egan, and the one I hit is his father, Frank. The third one is Frank's brother Burt. They run the Bar E spread in the southern end of Sunset

Valley, where my family ranch is, and there is a big family of them. Frank has a couple more sons, Buck and Ezra, and Burt has a son, Chris although Chris ain't around at the moment. They are trying to run my folks out, and I got back here before the shooting started. Things have warmed up some since I showed up, and I made a bad mistake riding into town alone tonight, but my sister Tilda didn't show up back at the ranch after coming to town this morning, and knowing what the Egan outfit is like, I had to come looking for her.'

Boots thudded on the sidewalk and a tall figure appeared from the shadows to their right. Halloran caught a glimpse of a law star glinting on the newcomer's chest and eased his pistol back into its holster.

'It's Joe Kett, the sheriff.' Deacon was under average height and of slight build, but fast with a gun. Dressed in range garb, he had a yellow neckerchief tied at his throat. His Stetson was pushed back off his forehead to reveal sun-bleached, yellow hair, and his usually cheerful face was set grimly.

'What is going on here?' Kett demanded. The glare of a lamp highlighted his ageing features. He was well into his fifties — leathery face, thin with high cheek bones and a long nose. His broad forehead overshadowed narrowed eyes, and a tight slash of a mouth was slightly askew above a prominent chin. He was wearing a dark suit with a cartridge belt buckled around his slim waist. 'Hell, it's you, Jeff!' he exclaimed in a husky voice. 'Who has been shot?'

'Rufus Egan,' Deacon replied. 'He jumped me when I walked into the saloon. Frank and Burt dragged me out, fixing to string me up, and walked slap-bang into my pard, Clint Halloran. Rufus ain't likely to die, and the other two are just laid out, but I'm sure getting mighty impatient about the way the Egans are always pushing for trouble.'

'I told you not to come into town

when the Egans are around,' Kett grated. 'I got enough on my plate without you tangling with them whenever you chance to meet. How the hell can I maintain law and order when you Sunset Valley folk can't live peaceable?'

'Tilda didn't come home from town, Sheriff, so I came looking for her,' Jeff said, forcing patience into his voice. 'Have you seen her around?'

'Sure did. She was on the street with Josie Wenn this afternoon. I told her to make it home before dark.' Kett bent over the two Egan men and checked them. He straightened and looked at the wounded Rufus but did not approach him. 'You say Rufus ain't dead?' he demanded.

'He's still breathing,' Halloran replied. 'A couple of weeks will see him back on his feet, if you've got a good doctor in town.'

The sheriff regarded Halloran in silence for some moments, and then exhaled in a heavy sigh. 'So you're Halloran, huh?' he observed. 'Jeff has been talking about you ever since he got back from his travels. He reckoned you would take this county apart when you showed up, and you ain't wasted any time getting started, huh? Well I ain't gonna stand for any two-bit gun hand coming in here and shooting up the local population.'

'It was self defence,' Halloran said. 'You ain't got a law against that, have you?'

'We got laws against a lot of things,' Kett replied. 'So where in hell has Tilda got to? You better slope outa here, Jeff, before any more Egans show up. I saw Mack Egan in town this afternoon, and I don't reckon he went home before dark. You scoot off back to the ranch and I'll look for Tilda. She can spend the night at my place. I wouldn't want her riding out to Big D alone after dark. She should have known better. My Martha will take care of her, and we'll send her home tomorrow.'

'I can't do that, Sheriff, and you know it,' Jeff replied sharply. 'As big as I am, Pa would skin me alive if I didn't take Tilda back with me.'

Halloran was watching the two unwounded Egans, who were coming back to their senses. His right hand dropped to the butt of his holstered gun when Frank Egan reached into a pocket as he sat up. Halloran caught the glint of reflected lamp light on a long blade and stepped forward to kick at the hand grasping it. His dusty toe connected with a thick wrist and the knife flew from Frank's grasp. The sheriff uttered a mild curse and drew his pistol. He slammed the barrel against Frank's head. Halloran winced at the sickening thud which emanated from the contact. Frank subsided instantly.

'You know it ain't us Deacons causing the trouble around the county,' Jeff said through clenched teeth. 'You talk about law and order, Sheriff, but you ain't giving us Deacons a fair crack of the whip. The Egans are getting away with everything short of murder, and the way this affair is turning out it won't be long before they add killing to their list.'

'I'm doing my best,' Kett growled. 'You tell Asa to come into town Thursday afternoon. I'll have Frank Egan do the same, and we'll see if we can't settle their differences without the violence. Luckily, no one has been killed yet, so this helling around has got to stop before the whole shebang gets out of hand.'

'Stop the Egans and there will be no more trouble,' Jeff said. 'We ain't to blame for what is going on. We're only fighting for our rights.'

Kett turned his head to peer into the shadows along the sidewalk when he heard the sound of approaching footsteps. Halloran saw a tall, thin figure appear.

'So you heard the shot, Doc,' Kett greeted. 'I was about to send for you.'

'I'd just sat down to supper,' the doctor replied. 'Who is it this time?'

'Rufus Egan.' Kett stifled a sigh.

'I could have guessed that, seeing Jeff

here.' The doctor's gaze flitted to Halloran. 'I'm Doc Woollard,' he introduced. 'Which side of the fence are you on in this dispute?'

'He's Clint Halloran, Doc,' Jeff cut in. 'My saddle pard. He's here to give me a hand against the polecats trying to steal us blind. If you think the trouble so far is bad then wait until Clint gets to work cleaning up.'

'You'd do well to let the sheriff try for peace his way,' Halloran said. 'The last thing anyone wants is an all-out range war.'

'The Egans want it,' Jeff declared. 'They've got the bad end of the valley and figure to take over our spread. That's all there is to it. The Deacons aren't pushing for trouble. We're happy with what we've got, and if the Egans don't pull in their horns then nothing but hot lead will put an end to this trouble.'

'Once you hit that particular trail there ain't no going back, Jeff,' Kett observed.

'Tell that to the Egan bunch,' Jeff

rasped. 'They are the ones on the prod.'

'You'd better hunt up Tilda and get on back to the ranch,' Kett turned his attention to the two men on the ground. 'Come on, Frank, Burt, on your feet and head for the jail. I'll put you behind bars until Jeff has pulled out of town. Doc, bring Rufus along to the office when he's able to move.'

Frank and Burt Egan got to their feet. Halloran observed them closely. They were dark skinned men, unkempt, bearded, with black hair and feral brown eyes. They returned Halloran's gaze with interest as the sheriff hustled them away, their faces set with grim expressions.

'I'd better see if Tilda is at the Wenn house with Josie,' Jeff said worriedly. 'I need to get back to the spread because the Egans have a bee in their bonnets about causing a ruckus as soon as it gets dark. If they ain't shooting up our spread then they are trying to steal our cattle.'

Halloran followed Deacon along the

sidewalk to the residential part of the street, and they reached a neat wooden frame house with a white picket fence out front surrounding a wide stretch of well tended garden. Two trees had been planted to give shade to the big front window of the building, and lamp light filtered from a front room to illuminate a porch that gave access to the front door.

A girl in a white dress stood up on the porch as Jeff opened the gate.

'Hi, Jeff,' she called in a pleasant tone. 'Tilda didn't say you would come calling this evening.'

'Howdy, Josie,' Deacon replied. 'I'm looking for Tilda. She came into town today to see you.'

'She did, and we spent the day together, but Tilda left early because she wanted to be on home range before sundown.' Alarm sounded in Josie's attractive tone. 'Say, you don't think something bad has happened to her, do you?' she demanded.

'What makes you say that?' Jeff asked.

'We bumped into Mack Egan this afternoon, and he was mighty persistent in pressing his attention on Tilda — wouldn't take no for an answer when she refused to walk out to the river with him.'

'Did she go with him?' Jeff demanded.

'No. She turned him down flat. But, you know, Mack isn't as bad as the rest of his family. I think he genuinely likes Tilda.'

'Yeah, as a snake likes its prey,' Deacon grated.

'How did Tilda get into town?' Halloran asked impatiently. 'Cut out the pleasant talk, Jeff, and let's find your sister.'

'She rode in,' Deacon replied. 'Say, if she is still in town then her horse should be in the livery barn. Let's take a look-see.'

'I walked to the barn with her,' Josie said.

'And did you see her ride out of town?' Halloran asked. He glanced around without realizing he was watching his surroundings and his right hand

17

was close to the butt of his holstered pistol.

Josie shook her head as she studied Halloran's tall figure. He was impressed by her beauty. She was tall and slender in a white dress. Her long black hair framed an oval face and she was good looking, with a pert nose and alert brown eyes.

'Who are you?' she queried.

'This is Clint Halloran,' Deacon introduced. 'Clint, meet Josie Wenn. Her father owns the general store.'

'Ah. I've heard a lot about you, Mr Halloran,' Josie said. 'Since he came home to this trouble, Jeff has talked of you and nothing else.'

'And the first thing he did when he showed up was save me from the Egans,' Jeff cut in. 'They were fixing to string me up when they got the drop on me.'

'Let's get back to Tilda,' Halloran said. 'Did you see her ride out of town, Miss Wenn?'

'No, I didn't.' Josie shook her head.

'My pa called to me as we were about to fetch her horse and I left Tilda at the barn door. I did look into the barn after my pa left me, but her horse was gone so I figured she had left, and I went on home. Now I wish I had been more alert. What if Mack Egan was waiting in the barn for her? He has acted like that around me, but I always made it clear that I wasn't interested in him.'

'Are you saying Tilda is interested in him?' Jeff demanded.

'Mack is a handsome man,' Josie countered.

'Let's look around town,' Halloran cut in. 'If Mack Egan is still around we can look him up and talk to him.'

'I'll do more than talk to him if he's harmed Tilda,' Deacon said angrily. 'I've had just about enough of the Egans swaggering around the county. I'll see you later, Josie.' He turned away and set off back along the street. 'I guess we better check the saloons,' he said to Halloran. 'And the Egans have got a shack outside of town where they lay up when they are too drunk to get back to Bar E.'

'I hope you find Tilda safe and well,' Josie called after them. 'Perhaps she rode home by the Turner spread to see Eva. She was talking about visiting Eva soon, and she might have decided to stay there overnight.'

'We'll check it out,' Deacon replied. 'But since this trouble began Tilda has made a point of getting home before dark, and if I have to turn this town inside out to find her then I'll do just that.'

They checked out the saloons without locating Mack Egan, and Deacon paused at the door of the law office, his face grim as he peered through a window.

'I'd better tell the sheriff what I've learned before we check out the Egan shack,' he decided.

Halloran remained in the background when they entered the office. Frank and Burt Egan were seated on chairs in front of the battered wooden desk at the rear of the office, and they were drinking whiskey from a bottle which the sheriff had apparently provided.

'So this is the kind of treatment you're dishing out to troublemakers!' Deacon said in surprise. 'You tell me to get out of town soon as I can, and then bring those two polecats in here and likker them up. So whose side are you on, Sheriff?'

'It ain't how it looks, Jeff,' Kett replied, shaking his head. 'I'm trying to make the Egans see the error of their ways, and there is nothing like a swig of whiskey to oil their tongues. I told you to get out of town and stay out. Why are you still around? Are you looking for trouble?'

Deacon explained and Kett shook his head.

'Tilda won't come to any harm if she's gone off with Mack Egan,' he said. 'Mack was telling me only the other day how much he likes her.'

'Then he's a danged fool,' Frank Egan rasped.

'Do you think we want Tilda to

tangle with any of you Egans?' Deacon demanded. 'I'd sooner see her dead than that.'

'We'll put a stop to Mack soon as we can,' Frank Egan snarled. 'We don't want one of ours getting ideas about a Deacon gal.'

'And we'll chase you Deacons clear out of the valley.' Burt Egan glared at the sheriff. 'You're wasting your time with peacemaking, Kett. We've got a right to that valley, and we're gonna take it over.'

'We'll be ready and waiting for you when you try,' Deacon rasped. 'Come along any time you feel like it.'

Halloran regarded Frank and Burt Egan and decided they were not bluffing. All the signs were that there would be lethal conflict between the two families, and he had turned up just in time to become embroiled in it. He looked at Jeff's angry face, aware that it was too late for any kind of peace keeping, and the sheriff's expression indicated that the lawman was of a similar mind. But before the action started there was the matter of Tilda Deacon's apparent disappearance. Halloran reached out and touched Jeff's shoulder.

'We'd better start looking for Tilda,' he said.

'Sure.' Jeff turned away. 'We can come back to stomp these polecats any time. If they want a fight then they can have it, with no holds barred. They over-stepped the mark tonight, Sheriff, so keep them locked up because they'll be dead by morning if you turn them loose.'

'Put a curb on your tongue, Jeff,' Kett advised. 'There ain't any percent-age in talking war. Lay off until I've tried to jaw some sense into these two. I'll keep them in jail for a few days if that is what it will take to stop them running wild, but you and your family will have to do your bit to help keep the peace. Go on back to your spread and tell Asa what I'm saying. Anything will be better than bloodshed, and anyone with a grain of sense will see the truth in my words.'

Halloran opened the street door and Jeff stepped out to the sidewalk, shaking his head at the sheriff's advice. With his usual caution, Halloran glanced quickly around the darkened street, and reached out to grasp Deacon's arm when he caught a quick movement in the shadows to his right. He thrust his pard aside violently, dropped to one knee as he palmed his pistol, and the next instant the peace of the town was rocked by a violent spate of shooting. Muzzle flame split the shadows and heavy echoes fled across the street.

Deacon groaned as a slug slashed across the top of his left shoulder. Halloran felt the powerful tug of a bullet boring through his leather holster, and his .45 blasted a quick reply as he levelled the weapon for action. He sprawled flat when a storm of hot lead splattered around him.

2

Halloran triggered his .45, aiming for the gun flashes across the street. He noted three guns shooting at them, and his tension fled as action burgeoned. The hammering guns sent harsh echoes crashing through the shadows. A man's voice, raised in sudden agony, testified to the accuracy of his shooting, and an indistinct figure pitched sideways and hit the dust. He rolled to his right and came up into the aim, his gun blasting as the muzzle covered the shadows where gun flame was erupting. He could hear bullets smacking into the ground around his lean body but ignored the threat, intent only upon cutting down the odds of the murderous trio throwing lead.

Jeff was shooting rapidly, and before Halloran was quite ready for it the action died away. A second man fell to the ground and, as gun echoes faded, Halloran's keen ears picked up the sound of receding footsteps in an alley opposite the jail. He got up on one knee, gun ready, and covered their surroundings.

'Are you OK, Jeff?' he demanded.

'I collected a bullet burn on my left shoulder,' Deacon replied, 'but it won't inconvenience me any. So the shooting has started! Well, it has been a long time coming, and now we can get to work. Cover me, Clint, and I'll take a look-see at those coyotes. I guess they are some of the Egan outfit.'

'Hey, Jeff, I'll handle this.' The sheriff called from the doorway of the law office and his harsh voice echoed across the street.

'You couldn't handle a barn dance,' Deacon replied. 'All you ever do is talk out against shooting. But now it has started, and I'm on the wrong end of it. So you better stay out of this, Sheriff. It's too late for talk now. A fight is being pushed on us.'

Halloran watched the shadows as Jeff got to his feet and went forward with levelled gun to where two silent figures were sprawled in the dust. Sheriff Kett emerged from the law office carrying a lantern, and hurried to the spot where Deacon had paused. Together they bent over one of the figures, and Halloran, his gun raised in readiness, covered them against further attack.

'I don't know this one,' Jeff said. 'Heck, he's a stranger. Let's look at the other one.'

The lantern moved on a couple of yards and then stopped again. Halloran went forward and paused at Jeff's side. He looked down at a bearded face that was composed in death.

'Another stranger,' Jeff said. 'What the hell is going on? Do you reckon the Egans have brought in some hired help?'

'You don't know that, Jeff,' Kett said quickly. 'Why don't you go home like I said and leave me to handle this?'

'You can do whatever you think is

27

right, but I've got a sister to find,' Jeff replied tensely. 'And I better find her safe and sound or there won't be an Egan left alive around here come sunup. Clint, let's check out the Egan shack.'

Halloran glanced at the sheriff's face as he followed Jeff along the street. Kett was shaking his head despairingly, clearly out of his depth in this situation. Jeff moved fast, almost at a run, and Halloran hurried to catch up with his pard.

'Take it easy, Jeff,' Halloran advised. 'Don't go off half-cocked.'

'I've got to find Tilda,' Jeff replied.

'You don't know that she hasn't already reached the ranch,' Halloran countered. 'Josie said her horse was gone from the barn so Tilda must have ridden out. She could be at home now, and if she is you'll be raising hell for nothing. You know you won't get anywhere acting like a mad bull.'

'I'm aware of that but my sister is involved and I know what the Egans are capable of. I ain't leaving town till I've clapped eyes on Tilda.'

'So where is the Egan shack?' Halloran demanded.

Jeff led the way along the street, his boots pounding the boardwalk; lamp light glinted on the long barrel of his .45. They reached the edge of town where the sidewalk ended, and were faced by a collection of shacks and cabins where townsfolk lived out their lives. The shadows were dense at this end of the street, and dim lantern lights were showing in some of the dusty windows of the crowded shanties.

'It's this way.' Jeff hastened between two shacks, and tripped over a pile of trash concealed in the shadows. He got to his feet, cursing, and blundered on, impelled by the thought of what might be happening to his sister. Halloran followed closely, his eyes narrowed to pierce the darkness. They passed a shack and heard two voices raised in argument. Halloran grimaced, for one of the voices was female, and it was raging against some injustice inflicted by a male.

Jeff slowed abruptly in front of a cabin and Halloran drew abreast of him. A horse was standing hip shot, tied to a post, its head low. Jeff swore softly as he patted the animal.

'This is Tilda's horse,' he said. 'So what the hell is she doing here? She knows better than to hang around town after sundown, and with an Egan.'

'Take it easy,' Halloran advised. 'You might stir up a hornets' nest if you go blundering in. You don't know who is inside so watch out.'

Jeff approached the lighted window in the front of the cabin. A piece of sacking had been drawn across the dusty pane, concealing the interior of the building. He muttered under his breath and turned to the door, which opened to his touch. He paused for a moment, then thrust the door wide and lunged inside, his gun lifting. Halloran followed closely, holding his pistol ready.

They both halted quickly at the sight

of the peaceful domestic scene before them. A man and a woman were seated at a rough wooden table, eating supper, and the smell of the cooked food twitched at Halloran's nostrils, making him aware of his own hunger. The young woman paused in the act of lifting a fork to her mouth and froze in the movement, staring aghast at the two men on the threshold. The man leapt to his feet, overturning his chair in his haste, and his right hand snatched at the pistol in the holster on his right hip.

'Don't pull it, Egan!' Jeff rasped. 'What the hell is going on here? Tilda, what are you doing eating with a damned Egan while some of his family were fixing to stretch my neck?'

Mack Egan dropped his right hand to his side. He was tall and slim, with dark hair which was greased and slicked back. He was wearing good clean range clothes — obviously his best attire. He was good looking, clean shaven, and had made an effort with his appearance. Tilda Deacon was a pretty girl, with blonde hair brushed back off her face. Her features resembled Jeff's. An expression of annoyance crossed her face and her blue eyes narrowed as she dropped her fork with a clatter.

'What are you doing in town, Jeff?' she demanded.

'Looking for you; that's what,' he replied. 'I've been worried sick about you, thinking all sorts of bad things had happened to you. Josie said she thought you had ridden out of town earlier, but here you are, acting as though you are at a picnic. What the hell are you doing with an Egan? You know they are fixing to run us out of the valley. They've been causing trouble for us, and shooting has started. So what's with you?'

'Mack ain't like that,' Tilda replied. 'He doesn't hold with what his family is doing. Just get out of here, Jeff, and leave us be. I'm entitled to see whom I please, and I get enough slanging at home from Pa without you riding herd on me too.'

'You should have more thought for

the rest of us,' Jeff retorted. 'There are some of us who will be dying soon. Come on home with me now and I won't tell Pa about this.'

Halloran watched the play between brother and sister, and read the significance between their words. He kept Mack Egan under close observation.

'I'm not going back to the ranch until I've finished my supper,' Tilda said obstinately. 'Go to Baxter's saloon, and when I come for you there we can ride home together.'

'Nothing doing!' Jeff shook his head. 'You'd better do like I say. Pa would skin you alive if he heard you were mixing with an Egan.'

'I ain't mixed up in the trouble you're getting,' Mack Egan said. 'All I want is a quiet life, and I'm not gonna pull my gun on anyone unless it is in self defence. We're not all branded with the same iron.'

'Do you think I would take your word on anything?' Jeff demanded.

'How come you are skulking around with Tilda? Your family is on the war path for no good reason, and we'll have to fight to save ourselves. So where does that leave you, standing in the middle? If you don't want to fight you'll have to get out before shooting starts. But I guess I know where you'll be when the smoke is flying.'

'I've been telling Tilda the only thing we can do is pull out,' Mack said quietly, 'but she doesn't wanta leave her family. She says blood is thicker than water and she can't walk out. If I could make her see sense we would be long gone, I can tell you.'

Jeff turned on his sister. 'Do you have any feelings for him?' he demanded.

'Sure I do.' Tilda's chin came up and her eyes glinted defiantly. 'Listening to you, Jeff, makes me realize just how bad this situation really is. There's no way out for any of us while you are so keen to fight.'

'I came home to put a stop to the trouble,' Jeff snapped, 'not start it, and I haven't put a foot wrong since I got here. When I arrived I found the Egans out in force, rustling stock and playing up hell on the range. So where do you get off accusing me of pushing for a fight? And the shooting has already started. We killed a couple of strangers a few minutes ago. They cut loose at us when we came out of the law office, and I don't doubt they've been brought in by the Egans.'

Halloran saw Mack Egan's expression change at Jeff's words and he stepped in close to Egan and whisked the gun out of the youngster's holster.

'I got a feeling this Egan knows something about those strangers,' Halloran said briskly. 'I saw his face change, Jeff, when you mentioned them. He knows what is going on.'

'Is that so? Well we'll soon get at the truth.' Jeff cocked his pistol and levelled it at Mack Egan.

Tilda uttered a cry of desperation and lunged forward to grasp her brother's gun arm. The hair-triggered weapon exploded when Jeff's finger jerked spasmodically at the unexpected attack, and smoke flared from the weapon. Mack Egan cried out in agony and pitched to the floor. Jeff threw his sister off. Halloran bent over Egan and saw blood staining the youngster's shirt front. He ripped open the sodden material to expose a bullet hole in the right side of Egan's chest.

'It looks like he needs the doc,' Halloran observed.

Tilda screamed at Jeff as she dropped to her knees beside Egan. She produced a handkerchief and dabbed at the blood welling up out of the wound. Halloran grasped her elbow, lifted her to her feet, and she looked up at him with shock-filled eyes.

'Run and fetch the doc,' Halloran said firmly.

Tilda nodded and hurried to the door. She departed swiftly, leaving the door open. Halloran looked at Jeff's troubled face.

'It looks like you've let this trouble

become personal, pard,' Halloran observed, 'and that ain't the way to come out on top.'

'Of course it's personal,' Jeff replied, shaking his head. 'My family is involved, and I was about to get my neck stretched when you showed up. I don't reckon there is any other way I can handle this. The shooting has already started, and it won't stop until we Deacons are all down in the dust or the Egans have been shot to hell.'

Halloran glanced towards the door when he heard a sound outside. Tilda appeared in the doorway, and she was followed closely by two men. Halloran saw that both men were holding drawn pistols, and slapped his right hand to the butt of his weapon. One of the men pushed Tilda to the floor and started shooting. Jeff went down sideways, his gun appearing in his hand. Halloran triggered his Colt and the cabin was rocked by heavy detonations.

The foremost man stopped as if he had walked into the side of a barn. His gun spilled from his hand as a slug smacked against his breast bone and he fell limply as his life ran out of him like water out of a hole in a bucket. Jeff fired from his position on the floor and the second man spun away, pitched forward on to his face, and lay unmoving. The interior of the cabin was filled with gun smoke. Halloran yawned to relieve the pressure in his ears. He covered the doorway, ready for more trouble, but the action was over.

'Are you OK, Jeff?' Halloran called.

'Yeah.' Deacon got to his feet, dragging Tilda upright. She staggered when he let go of her elbow. 'So what happened?' he demanded. 'Where in hell did those two come from?'

'They were outside the cabin,' Tilda replied shakily. 'One grabbed me. They said they were friends of the Egans, and forced me back inside.' She looked down at the two men and shook her head. 'I don't know who they are. I have never seen them before in my life. Why are we getting all this trouble, Jeff?'

'More strangers,' Jeff commented. 'I think we'd better get out of here and split the breeze back to the ranch.'

'I'm not leaving Mack here like this,' Tilda protested. 'We've got to get help for him.'

'There'll be help pretty quick,' Halloran observed. 'Someone will have heard the shooting.'

'Get outside and grab your horse, Tilda,' Jeff said sharply, 'and quit stalling. We've got to get moving.'

'Why don't you two go back to the ranch and leave me here?' Tilda said wearily.

'That's a fool question.' Jeff grasped Tilda's arm and forced her to the door. He peered outside, his pistol raised and ready for action.

Halloran followed closely, closing the door at his back and cutting off the stream of light shafting out of the cabin. Figures moved in the surrounding shadows but there was no shooting, and then the sheriff's voice challenged them.

'Hold it, Jeff,' Kett called. 'What was that shooting about?'

'I've got Tilda with me,' Jeff replied from a corner of the cabin. 'A couple of strangers busted in, tried to take us, and we killed them. Mack Egan is inside. He needs the doc. He was shot accidentally.'

'Leave town now and I'll be out to the ranch in the morning to talk about this,' Kett replied.

Halloran raised his eyebrows at the sheriff's words, and covered Jeff and Tilda around to the back of the cabin; Tilda led her horse and Jeff remained at her side. Halloran brought up the rear, his gun in his hand, and they cleared the area without incident. They reached the main street; Halloran was surprised that there was not more interest in the shooting that had occurred. He collected his sorrel from the front of the saloon and Jeff led the way to the livery barn to get his horse.

They rode out of town at a canter and headed north. Halloran rode beside the silent Tilda, who spurred her horse into a fast run as soon as they cleared the street. Jeff protested at the girl's recklessness, but she ignored him and continued at a breakneck pace. Halloran frowned at the girl's behaviour. Jeff rode in beside his sister and grasped her reins.

'Take it easy, Tilda,' he rebuked. 'Mack Egan won't die from that wound, and you can't help the situation any by breaking your neck.'

'I'll come back to town tomorrow to see how Mack is,' Tilda responded.

'I reckon Pa will have something to say about that when he hears about the events in town tonight,' Jeff retorted. He turned to Halloran. 'Thanks for backing my play back there, Clint. We've got to be careful how we cover the last miles to our spread. The Egan ranch lies between us and it. Most of the trouble has come from friction between the spreads because we have to cross Egan range to get to town or back to the ranch. The only way around it is

41

to ride an extra twenty miles each time to stay clear of their boundaries. It's our right to use the trail in and out, but now the smoke has started flying it will be a different can of beans. The Egans patrol the area where we cross their grass, and shooting will surely start now.'

'From what I've picked up since I hit town I'd say you need to work closely with the sheriff,' Halloran mused. 'He's trying to prevent a shooting war, and you would go along with him if you wanted to avoid bad trouble. But I've got a sneaking feeling you want the war to start, Jeff. Am I right?'

'Yeah! I've thought long and hard about this situation, and I've come to the conclusion that the only way to handle it is to shoot the whole damn bunch of Egans. They ain't ever gonna let up wanting our spread, and if we don't get them first then one fine morning we're gonna wake up and find them on the warpath and breathing down our necks. My pa ain't keen on pushing for a fight. But I've seen enough action in the past to know how these things explode when you ain't ready for them.'

Halloran nodded. 'Count me in whichever way you decide to jump,' he said.

'I was hoping you'd say that, pard.' Jeff's teeth gleamed in the night as he grinned. 'Now you're here, and willing, we can make plans to jump the Egans and put an end to this trouble once and for all.'

They rode across fine rangeland through the deceptive shadows of the night. A half moon was sailing across a high and wide sky, providing them with ample light to observe their surroundings. The range was silent, still, and the thud and beat of their hoofs sounded ghostly in a seemingly unreal world. Miles slipped by under the willing legs of their mounts. Halloran studied the country through which they rode, his thoughts roving. He was satisfied that the Egans were troublemakers, and the

Deacons had every right to protect themselves and their range. The Deacons were peaceable folk who would fight to the last drop of their blood to defend their rights in this untamed land.

Twelve miles from town they reached a wide stream running out of the high ground to the north, and they approached a wide valley that stretched in a lazy curve to the north-west. Jeff reined in and peered around.

'Sunset Valley,' he said in an aside to Halloran. 'We've got to be careful from here on in. Those damn Egans will be out and about, I shouldn't wonder. They never miss a chance these days to give us trouble. Tilda, ride carefully; and you better keep your hand close to your gun, Clint.'

'There is movement on the crest to the left,' Halloran observed. 'Three riders are coming out of those trees.' He dropped his right hand to the butt of his pistol and straightened his shoulders, ready for trouble. 'Play it by ear, Jeff,' he advised.

'OK. But be ready to start shooting,' Jeff replied. He reined in as the riders approached, his left hand holding his reins while his right hand remained close to his holstered pistol. 'I'm not giving an inch any more,' he said bitterly. 'I have bent over backwards to keep the peace, but all that is done right now. If the Egans want trouble then they'll sure as hell get it. Let them step over the mark this time and it'll mean shooting for sure.'

Halloran straightened his shoulders and loosened his gun in its holster. He sat his mount on Jeff's left and waited stoically. The newcomers approached at a canter, moving apart slightly as they drew closer. They reined in only feet away and Halloran sensed their belligerence. Two of them were gripping the butts of their holstered guns and seemed to be straining with eagerness to draw. Halloran felt the old familiar tensions run through his veins as he waited for the first hostile movement which would trigger smoky action.

'Where do you reckon you're going?' one of the trio demanded.

'You know exactly where we are going, Zack Egan,' Jeff replied. 'We're heading home. What are you doing out here in the night, challenging honest travellers? Anyone would think we didn't have the right to cross this range.'

'You don't have that right any more,' Zack Egan replied with a short, cynical laugh. 'The trail is closed. You Deacons have got to go around by the long way now.'

'Do you figure you can make that stick?' Jeff demanded.

'Try us!' Naked challenge sounded in the curt tone of Zack Egan's voice.

'You're gonna have to make the first move,' Jeff grated. 'If I shoot anyone it will be in self defence.'

Halloran was straining his eyes to make out details of the trio confronting them. Two were big men, dark faced and looking like brothers. Jeff had called one of them Zack Egan, so here were two more of the opposing family, on the prod and with no intention of backing down. The third man was small, slightly built, and wore two guns on crossed belts. He looked like a snake about to strike, and spoke sharply out of the side of his mouth.

'Zack, I smell gun trouble!' he rapped. 'That stranger with Deacon is a gun hawk, and he's ready to pull his iron. I can smell his kind a mile off.'

'So you have brought in a hired gun, Deacon!' Zack Egan rasped.

'He's a long-time pard of mine come up from Texas for a visit,' Jeff replied. 'Keep your long nose out of this business, Sloan. Now get out of our way, Zack, or pull your gun.'

'Let me take him, Zack,' Sloan said.

'You men make me sick to my stomach,' Tilda said sharply. 'Throwing challenges and threatening peaceful folk going about their lives. Isn't it tough enough on the range without all this trouble? Why can't you all live in peace?

There's enough room in this valley for everyone.'

'Stay out of this, gal!' Zack growled. 'If you don't want trouble then get out of the valley. And that goes for the whole damn bunch of you Deacons.'

'Mack never wanted trouble but he was shot in town tonight,' Tilda continued.

'Mack was shot?' Zack rasped. 'Which one of you murdering Deacons did it?'

'It was an accident,' Jeff said harshly. 'And he ain't dead.'

Halloran felt a tingle in the fingers of his right hand. Sloan's horse took a sudden pace forward under the pressure of the gunman's left hand on his reins and leather creaked. There was enough light on the range for Halloran to see gun hands clearly, and he waited for any sudden movement. It came from Sloan, who reached for a holstered gun with his left hand. Starlight glinted on metal as the big .45 was snatched out of its holster. Halloran moved as if governed by Sloan's thought processes. He palmed his gun, cocked it, and fired instantly.

The crash of the shot smashed the brooding silence of the range and a gun flash spurted. Sloan jerked backwards in his saddle and then pitched sideways out of leather. Halloran shifted his aim, and caught both Egans in the act of reaching for their guns.

'Don't do it,' Halloran warned. 'You wanted blood and you've got it. Sloan is dead.'

'Get rid of your guns,' Jeff rapped. 'One at a time and do it slow.'

Zack Egan sat for a moment before lifting his pistol out of its holster with the index finger and thumb of his right hand. He dropped the weapon to the ground.

'Now you, Ezra,' Jeff continued. 'Don't make a mistake or you're dead.' He waited until Ezra Egan had complied, and then nodded. 'Now throw Sloan back in his saddle and get him out of here. After this you better be ready to fight on sight, because we ain't gonna take any more from you Egans. You've pushed us to the limit, and now you'll have to take the consequences.'

Halloran watched intently as Zack Egan dismounted and loaded the dead gunman on to his horse. There was no fight in either Egan right now, and they were silent as they turned away and rode back into the trees on the crest. Halloran shook his head, aware that the shooting had not ended the dispute. The death of a hired gun was just the beginning, and soon the shooting would begin in earnest and go on until one side or the other was wiped out . . .

3

Jeff slapped the rump of Tilda's horse when the Egans had disappeared under the trees and the animal started forward rapidly. They rode on, following the stream north, and the silence of the range closed in about them. Halloran felt no pangs of conscience at having killed Sloan, for he understood why the Deacon family were in trouble. He knew from experience that the only way to beat such hard-nosed men as the Egans was to shoot them.

'You can see what I'm up against,' Jeff said shortly. 'I tried to talk peace but the Egans took that as a sign of weakness so I had to change my tune. But at least I know where we stand now. The war has started.'

'Pa won't be happy when you tell him what you've done today,' Tilda said angrily. 'You have talked of fighting ever since you came home. You should have stayed away, Jeff, and perhaps this trouble would have blown over.'

'You don't believe that for a moment,' Jeff said sharply. 'Do you think I like the idea of a range war? I know the signs, and what they tell me is that if we don't hit the Egans hard they will get the drop on us. This way, we have a chance of coming out on top.'

Halloran said nothing, but mentally agreed with Jeff, and his thoughts were hard as they continued through the night.

'The Egans have a tough crew that are ready to back any play,' Jeff said. 'I reckon they'll plan a visit to our place at night, but we are ready for them. I had to talk my pa into preparing for a fight; we have guards out so we shan't get caught napping.'

'I think you should have another talk with the sheriff,' Halloran mused.

Jeff shook his head. 'I don't think I'll get much help from that direction. You saw the way Kett was treating Frank and Burt Egan — feeding them whiskey! That tells me a lot about which way the law will jump when the shooting starts. And Kett has a bullying deputy named Dan Ramsey who should be behind bars himself instead of working for the law.'

'Ramsey is sweet on one of the Egan gals,' Tilda said sharply.

'Mattie Egan. She's Burt Egan's daughter,' Jeff added. 'There was a time when I was sweet on Mattie,' he continued. 'But I cut that dead because I couldn't stomach marrying into the Egan family.'

'You might have averted this trouble if you'd gone ahead with her,' Halloran observed.

Jeff laughed harshly. 'I did think about that, but figured the price was too high. Anyway, Ramsey doesn't seem to mind mixing with that brood of polecats, and we'll know for sure which side he'll be on when the smoke starts blowing.' He paused, and then added, 'No, I don't think I'll try and get the law on my side. We're gonna have to handle this ourselves.'

They continued through the shadows, following the stream. A high slope on their right reared up to throw a great dense shadow over part of the valley floor, and stands of timber dotted the skyline. Halloran liked what he could see, and wished he had arrived in daylight to pick out more details. There was an abundance of water and the grass was lush — a true cattleman's paradise. But there was a snag to the set-up — the Egans.

The stream angled to the north-west, and they followed it until the outline of a large house appeared on a stretch of high ground rising up out of the valley floor. Bright yellow lantern light threw a glow across the dusty yard in a cosy welcome. Halloran noted a motley collection of smaller buildings in the background.

'So this is the Deacon ranch,' Halloran observed.

'It sure is, and no Egan is ever gonna

set foot on it,' Jeff replied.

'I'll say amen to that,' Halloran commented.

They rode into the yard in front of the house and a low voice called a challenge from the shadows on the porch.

'It's OK, Ham,' Jeff replied. 'We're back from town. Come on out and show yourself. There's someone with me I want you to meet.'

A tall figure eased out of the shadows and came forward, gripping a rifle in his hands, his face shadowed by his wide-brimmed Stetson.

'So you found Tilda, huh?' he said. 'Pa is awful sore with you, Tilda, for disobeying him.'

The girl dismounted and trailed her reins. 'Don't nag, Ham. Take care of my horse for me.' She spoke angrily, and hurried into the house.

'Meet my pard Clint Halloran, Ham,' Jeff said. 'Clint, this is my brother Ham. He's two years older than me. Clint showed up in town just as Frank and

Burt Egan were fixing to stretch my neck, Ham.'

'So you found trouble,' Ham replied. 'I knew I shoulda ridden in with you. I'd have done more good at your side than wandering around here with a rifle, looking for polecats that ain't ever gonna show up. Say, I'm pleased to meet you, Clint. Jeff sure has talked a lot about you since he got home. I hope you know what you're getting yourself into.'

'I accidentally shot Mack Egan in town,' Jeff said. 'Then there were two men outside the law office, and then two more at the Egan shack on the edge of town — all strangers. And if that wasn't enough for one day, Clint killed Sloan when we were confronted by him and Zack and Ezra Egan when we reached their range.'

'Jeez! I sure wish I had been there!' Ham said excitedly. 'Is Mack Egan dead?'

Jeff explained in detail the incidents that had taken place earlier, and

Halloran looked around the yard, peering into the shadows, listening for suspicious sounds in the background; although he was satisfied that the night was peaceful he did not relax. He did not like the set-up facing the Deacons and sensed that they could not win a fight with the Egans unless they struck first, and hard and fast.

'You better go into the house before Pa tans Tilda's hide,' Ham said. 'He's been madder than a wet hen since sundown. He gave Tilda strict orders to be home before the sun set. But your news will make him even madder, I shouldn't wonder. Looks like the Egans are coming out of the woodwork, huh? I sure hope I get a chance at them before this fight is done. You said the other men you killed in town were strangers, huh?'

'Nobody seemed to know them.' Jeff moved towards the house. 'I got it figured that the Egans have brought in a bunch of gun hands to help them push us out. Come on, Clint. I want

57

you to meet my pa.'

'I'll take care of your horses,' Ham said. 'It'll help me pass the time.'

'You'd better keep your eyes skinned for trouble,' Jeff warned. 'Be careful, Ham.'

'I wish the Egans would come,' Ham replied.

Halloran followed Jeff into the house. Tilda was sitting at a long wooden table, her face set obstinately in open defiance. An old man, grey-bearded, with wide, stiff shoulders, was standing at the far end of the table, his face showing anger as he confronted his daughter. An older woman was sitting on a stiff-backed chair in a corner by the massive fireplace, and by her side was seated another young woman. Halloran ran his gaze over her and open admiration showed momentarily in his face.

'That's my sister Cora,' Jeff said. 'I was watching you, Clint, to get your reaction to her. Ain't she a beauty?'

Halloran nodded. Cora Deacon was

one of the loveliest women he had ever seen. Tall and shapely, she was wearing a fitted red shirt and denim pants. Dark, shoulder length hair framed her oval face, and her brown eyes lifted from the piece of knitting she was busily engaged with to survey Halloran as he looked at her.

'Cora, this is Clint Halloran, my good friend,' Jeff introduced. 'He's here to help us fight the Egans.'

'It would be better if he came to help find a solution to the trouble other than fighting with a gun,' Cora replied, and returned her gaze to her knitting.

Halloran, although rebuffed by the girl's tone, was unable to take his eyes off her.

'Pa, this is Clint Halloran,' Jeff continued, interrupting his father's tirade. 'We had some bad trouble in town, and Clint saved my life a couple of times. Now he's here we'll take the fight to the Egans, and find out how tough they are.'

'I warned you against pushing for

trouble.' Asa Deacon straightened and came around the table with outstretched hand. He paused in front of Halloran, his blue eyes steady. 'I'm glad you're on our side,' he remarked, shaking hands. 'It looks like we can't put off this trouble any longer. The Egans have been pushing for it, and they won't be satisfied until they are down in the dust.' He paused and looked at Jeff, then reached out and touched his son's left shoulder. 'You've been hurt,' he observed.

'It's just a scratch,' Jeff replied.

'What did Kett do about the shooting in town?' Asa asked.

'Not much.' Jeff glanced at Halloran. 'You saw the way Kett was acting in town, Clint,' he said. 'He arrested Frank and Burt Egan, who were fixing to string me up, but when we dropped into the jail a little later, he was giving them whiskey. If that doesn't show you which side the law is on then I don't know what will. You've got to come down off the fence, Pa, and make up your mind to the fact that we are going to have to fight to survive in this valley. I know the Egans will turn up here unexpectedly one day, and blood will run — our blood.'

'The shooting in town today is pushing us along a trail that has no future for anyone,' Asa Deacon said harshly. 'Maybe if I ride into town tonight and have a talk with Sheriff Kett we might be able to save something from this mess. But I've known for a long time that Kett won't go out of his way to help us any.'

'You'd likely get yourself killed,' Jeff responded, shaking his head. 'A bunch of strangers attacked us in town, and I'm thinking they were brought into this by the Egans.'

'We'll sleep on it then, and ride into town in the morning,' Asa decided. 'Cora, you and Tilda get supper ready. We'll have an early night, and come sunup we'll all ride into town to see the sheriff.'

The porch door was opened and

Ham Deacon stepped into the big room. 'I heard riders out on the range,' he said urgently. 'Sounded like six horses. They stopped some way out, and I reckon they are working their way in close right now. What are you gonna do about it, Jeff?'

'Put the lights out and everyone stay put and ready to fight,' Jeff replied without hesitation. 'I'll go outside and see what's doing. Don't shoot unless we are attacked, and be careful you don't shoot me.'

Halloran moved to the door behind Jeff and they slipped out to the porch as the lights in the big room were extinguished. The yard was heavily shadowed. They stood motionless, listening intently to the natural noises of the night. The moon was far over in the west, barely above the horizon, and starlight limned the drifting clouds being pushed eastward by the incessant breeze. The silence was intense. Halloran eased his pistol in its holster sensing a degree of hostility in the air that warned him trouble was present.

'I don't like it, Clint,' Jeff said. 'It is too quiet.'

'We're as ready as we'll ever be,' Halloran responded. 'I reckon the Egans have got to come probing to follow up on the trouble they caused around town.'

An owl hooted from the shadows around the barn to the left. Jeff drew his pistol, and the rasp of steel against leather was loud in the silence.

'That was no owl,' he hissed. 'I'll go along the left side of the house to the rear and take a look around the back yard. Keep an eye open here, Clint.'

'I'll watch the other side of the house from the end of the porch,' Halloran replied, and cocked his pistol.

Jeff walked to the end of the porch and stepped around the corner into total darkness. He strode along the side of the house, his gun ready, and paused at the rear corner overlooking the yard and the two barns, remaining in the cover of the corner. The shadows were impenetrable and he strained his ears for unnatural sound. When he heard the click of a steel shod hoof against a stone he cocked his pistol and restrained his breathing. A moment later he caught the sudden flare of a match being ignited in the nearest barn, and the next instant a pile of straw began burning furiously.

A figure was bending over the growing conflagration, and Jeff snapped a shot at the man, who spun and fell on his face as the echoes of the shot blasted through the silence. Two guns returned fire from a corner of the barn, and Jeff heard slugs smacking into the woodwork of the corner just above his head. He dropped to one knee and started shooting in earnest, aiming for muzzle flashes; another two guns joined in the fight from the second barn to the right.

Jeff counted five guns shooting from cover opposite, and stayed behind the corner as the full weight of fire sprayed around his position. Someone started shooting from inside the kitchen, using a rifle, and Jeff emptied his gun rapidly, intent on gaining the initiative. A moment later another weapon started shooting from the far rear corner of the house, and he guessed Halloran had bought into the action.

But the attacking fire was not sustained. It quickly dribbled away into an uneasy silence, and moments later Jeff heard the sound of receding hoofs out there in the night. When full silence came he started towards the barn where straw was blazing brightly. He was ready for trouble, but nothing happened as he crossed the yard and gained the shelter of the barn.

'Cover me from the kitchen,' Jeff shouted. 'I think they've pulled out but we won't take any chances.'

He ran into the barn and began to stamp on the burning straw. Halloran arrived seconds later, and between them they extinguished the blaze. Jeff turned to the inert figure lying on the floor. He struck a match, held the tiny flame close to the upturned face, and cursed softly when he saw that the dead man was a stranger.

'He's the fifth stranger we've killed today,' Jeff muttered as he blew out the match. 'I can't believe the Egans would bring in a bunch of gunnies — there are enough of them to handle this gun chore themselves. So what gives, Clint?'

Halloran shrugged. 'We'll get to the bottom of it in time,' he replied. 'What do you figure on doing now?'

'I'll ride over to the Egan spread and give them something to think about,' Jeff replied. 'They won't be expecting an attack tonight, and it might set them back a bit.'

'I was gonna suggest the same thing,' Halloran said. 'We'll ride together, pard.'

They returned to the house, which was still in darkness. Ham Deacon called from the kitchen doorway, his challenge ringing out across the darkened yard.

'They've gone,' Jeff replied. 'We're

coming in, Ham.'

They entered the house and went through to the big front living room. Asa lit a lamp. His face wore a worried expression as he listened to Jeff's explanation of what had happened.

'The sooner I get to town and talk with Kett the better,' Asa observed.

'That won't do any good,' Jeff countered. 'I've got a better idea. You stay put here on your guard with the outfit backing you while Clint and I ride over to the Egan place and give them something to think about.'

Asa shook his head. 'You know I can't agree to that, Jeff,' he said bitterly. 'It would be an open declaration of war.'

'Turn the other cheek, huh?' Ham demanded. His fleshy face was contorted with anger. 'I agree with Jeff, Pa. We should all ride over to the Egans and give them a bloody nose. It might stop them in their tracks.'

'It would only bring them out in force, and we couldn't win a stand-up battle with them,' Asa said. 'Let's do this my way, boys. I know I'm right.'

Jeff glanced at Halloran, who nodded slightly. He heaved a long sigh and shrugged his wide shoulders.

'OK,' he said. 'We'll play it your way, Pa. We'll ride into town tomorrow, talk to Kett, and after you realize that you'll get no help from the law we'll go for the Egans and teach them a lesson they won't forget.'

'Now you're talking,' Ham said excitedly.

'We'll go out and take a look around the spread,' Jeff continued. 'I wanta make sure no Egans are sneaking around out there. The rest of you better turn in and get some sleep. After this I reckon we'll have a lot of sleepless nights.'

Halloran led the way through to the kitchen, and he and Jeff left the house noiselessly to stand in the dense shadows of the back yard. They both listened intently and heard nothing but the natural noises of the night.

'What do you make of it, Clint?' Jeff asked. 'You've been in this kind of situation more times than I have. How does it strike you?'

'I'm thinking along the same lines you are,' Halloran replied in an undertone. 'I never saw men more prepared to fight than the Egans. They ain't gonna listen to reason nohow. If this was a job we'd bought into we'd go over to their spread right now and shoot holes in them before they could get around to coming in here with murder on their minds.'

'They've already come here,' Jeff observed, 'although I reckon it was just to test us. We sure gave them a bloody nose, so what do you expect them to do next?'

'Come back in force and wipe us out,' Halloran replied.

Jeff nodded. 'That's how I see it,' he agreed, his tone filled with despair. 'And I wish I could get Pa to see it my way. I'll have to go along with him though. We'll talk to Kett again, although it will be a complete waste of time, and afterwards we'll hit the Egans where it hurts most.'

'Now you're talking, pard,' Halloran said tensely. 'We've got a fight on our hands.'

Jeff looked around into the shadows, his thoughts harsh. He would not fight if he could find another way to solve their problems, but he knew only too well how the Egans were stacking up against his family, and he was not prepared to take chances with their lives.

'I'll stick around out here for a couple of hours,' Jeff mused. 'Perhaps you'll relieve me later. I want to get this trouble done with in the next couple of days, before the Egans have a chance to get themselves together. Tell Ham to show you to my bed, Clint, and get what rest you can. Tomorrow we hit the gun trail, and there'll be no rest for anyone until the smoke clears.'

Halloran nodded and re-entered the house. He found Tilda and Cora Deacon in the kitchen, preparing supper, and stood watching them. Tilda was in a bad mood, her movements quick and angry, but Cora seemed greatly preoccupied, her thoughts apparently elsewhere as she performed her mundane chores. She kept her head lowered and her intent gaze upon her hands. Halloran could sense her coldness, which seemed to be directed against him, and wondered at the undercurrents of emotions which gripped the different members of this family. He would do what he could to help out, but he had it figured that whatever he did, his actions would not be approved by all the Deacons, and he could not even guess at the outcome to the approaching fight, for this was not a family united in a common effort.

4

Jeff moved silently through the shadows at the rear of the ranch house. He could smell burned straw, and crossed to the barn where the dead stranger was still lying. His thoughts roamed over the situation and a sense of restlessness gripped him, impelled by frustration. He had been back from Texas a little more than two weeks, and in that time he had taken insults and aggravation from the Egans because, although he talked tough, he hoped to find a way out of the trouble without resorting to violence. But now he knew only too well that shooting was the only way to deal with them Egans.

He felt a sudden impulse to ride and went around to the corral and took his rope. He settled the loop on a black and saddled it, and then mounted and rode to the porch. Leaving the horse with trailing reins, he opened the front door and looked into the big room and motioned to Halloran to join him outside.

'I'm gonna take a ride into town and talk to the sheriff,' Jeff said.

'Want me to ride with you?' Halloran asked.

'I'd be happy to have you along, but I'd like it if you stuck around here, just in case the Egans show up again. I'll be back before morning. Don't tell anyone where I'm going.'

'OK. Just watch your step,' Halloran replied.

Jeff swung into his saddle, and when he was clear of the ranch he could feel relief welling up in his mind. He had felt uneasy when his father decided to ride into town the next day for he was afraid something bad might happen to the oldster, and he decided to ride into Plainsville, have another talk with Sheriff Kett, and if the lawman failed to act decisively then he would take drastic measures before the sun came up to settle the trouble between the Deacons and the Egans.

Jeff pushed the black into a lope that ate up the miles. The animal was fresh and willing. Jeff breathed deeply of the keen night air and watched his surroundings intently for he was crossing Egan range and there was always a danger of running into an ambush. But he saw nothing to cause worry and crossed the stream to follow the trail into Plainsville.

When the lights of the little town showed up in the distance, Jeff paused on the outskirts to study the main street. It was almost midnight and most of the townsfolk had retired, but he saw a light in the law office, and the big saloon was still open. He looked for horses, saw none, and rode around to the rear of the livery barn to check for Egan horseflesh. A single lantern burned inside the big barn but there was barely sufficient light to pick out details of the animals. He checked the stalls on foot and was satisfied that the

Egans had gone home for the night. His lips compressed as the thought came to him that perhaps the enemies of his family were massing now on the range for an attack on the Deacon ranch.

Jeff moved on across the back lots, leading his horse towards the law office. He tethered the black within easy reach of the back door of the jail and entered an alley at the side to head for the street door. He paused at a side window and peered into the office to see Kett seated at his desk. The sheriff was dozing, his elbows on the desk, his head in his hands; a pistol lay on the desk close to his right elbow. He was about to move on when the connecting door between the office and the cells was opened and a big, wide-shouldered man appeared.

It was Dan Ramsey, the county deputy sheriff, his law badge glinting on his chest. Jeff did not like the bullying deputy, partly because the lawman liked to throw his weight around, and because Ramsey always viewed him with contempt, being aware that Jeff lived by his gun. He watched the deputy cross the office to the street door and depart noisily. Sheriff Kett started up when the door slammed, and Jeff watched Ramsey pass the alley mouth and head off along the sidewalk towards the saloon.

The sheriff resumed his dozing and Jeff left the alley and entered the office, closing the door noiselessly. He stood before the desk for a moment, studying the sheriff. Kett had got old, he decided, and probably was not up to handling the kind of trouble now brewing in the county. The sheriff had been an excellent lawman many years before, but he had slowed considerably lately, and was no longer the force he had been, tending to spend more time in his office than out law-dealing.

'Sheriff,' he called softly, and Kett stirred and then opened his eyes and straightened.

'What in hell are you doing back in town, Jeff?' he demanded instantly. 'I thought I told you to stay away until

I've had a chance to look into your trouble. You'll only make matters worse by hanging around. The sight of you to the Egans is like a red rag to a bull. I managed to talk Frank and Burt out of acting outside of the law, and they went home a couple of hours ago.'

'I came in to report that our ranch was attacked by six riders,' Jeff said. 'They tried to set fire to one of the barns. One of them was killed and the others made a run for it.'

'The hell you say!' Kett shook his head wearily. 'Who got killed?'

'No one we know.' Jeff shrugged. 'There's a bunch of strangers operating around here, and you don't need to ask who has brought them in. It sure as hell ain't us Deacons. They've done nothing but toss lead at us since they showed up, and you're telling us to sit back and do nothing. You've got to come up with something better than that, Sheriff.'

'Frank and Burt denied knowing anything about strangers coming in,' Kett said doggedly.

'And you believe them despite the fact that those strangers are shooting at the Deacons. If we brought them in they would be shooting Egans, wouldn't they?'

'I ain't got any proof against anyone.' Kett's face was lined by worry. 'You know I can't act without evidence.'

'So you want to see some of my family stretched out dead before you'll believe the Egans are fixing to wipe us out, huh? Well, it ain't gonna work that way, Sheriff. Asa said he'll ride into town in the morning to talk to you, but you better have a lot more on the table to satisfy him than you got right now. We have the right to defend ourselves if we are attacked, like tonight, and you know that once the shooting starts in earnest it won't stop until one or the other side is finished.'

Kett shook his head and sighed heavily. 'You better talk to Ramsey about this,' he said. 'I've decided to take a back seat in this trouble. Ramsey is a younger man and he can stand the pace. As for me, I've had my fill trying to sort out the trouble in this county.'

'You mean the job has got too tough for you. Hell, you should quit and make room for a man who will stand up to the Egans, but don't put Ramsey in control. He's fixing to marry one of the Egan gals so we all know where his sympathies lie.'

'Ramsey will do the job just fine.' Kett waved a hand. 'Just get outa here and stop spoiling my sleep, Jeff. I'm tired of all this wrangling. If you can't live peaceably alongside the Egans then you'll have to do the other thing.'

Jeff stared at Kett in disbelief. He opened his mouth but closed it again without speaking, shook his head, and then turned to the door. He paused on the threshold before throwing a parting shot.

'You said it,' he rapped. 'Sure, we know what we've got to do. We also knew there would be no help coming from the kind of law you are running around here. So that's the way it will be.'

'Go back to your spread,' Kett said wearily. 'Any shooting you've got to do, don't do it inside of town limits. I'll come down hard on you Deacons if you spill blood around here.'

Jeff departed and slammed the door of the office. He stood for a moment, breathing heavily in anger, and his blood ran hot with fury. But now he knew exactly where he stood. He moved towards the big saloon, feeling in need of a beer. When he peered over the batwings into the saloon he was still so angry he barely noticed the occupants in the big room, and shouldered through the swing doors to stomp angrily to the bar. Only then did he look around with his customary caution, and alertness filtered into his mind when he saw Tom Dixon, the saloon owner, standing at the bar with two gun-hung strangers.

The bar tender, Al Sowerby, came along the bar to confront Jeff. His thin lips barely moved in his gaunt face when he asked, 'What'll it be?'

'Beer,' Jeff replied.

Sowerby slid a foaming pint glass along the polished bar with practised ease. He was a diminutive man with slim shoulders; a lightweight who did his job in sullen silence. But he glanced along the bar to where the obese Dixon was chatting with the two strangers, and cleared his throat to remark.

'I didn't expect you to show your face in here again after what happened earlier,' Sowerby said. 'Frank and Burt Egan were fixing to string you up when they dragged you out the door earlier.'

'They made a big mistake,' Jeff replied, his gaze on Dixon and the strangers, and he saw both strangers stiffen at the bar tender's words. One of the two seemed vaguely familiar and Jeff frowned as he tried to place the man, who stepped away from the bar and dropped his right hand to the butt of his holstered gun.

'What's your name, mister,' the stranger demanded.

'What's it to you?' Jeff countered.

'I'm Chris Egan, and I'm on the watch for any Deacon who sticks his nose inside of town limits, that's what. If Frank and Burt tangled with you earlier then you must be that two-bit gunnie Jeff Deacon.'

'Chris Egan!' Jeff exclaimed in a shocked tone. 'Hell, you boss a gang of bank robbers! How come the sheriff lets you run free around here? There's a price on your head for stealing and murder.'

'Kett can't stop us.' Egan laughed. 'Pull your gun, Deacon. You made a bad mistake coming in here. You're out of this fight as of now.'

'Hey, I don't want any shooting in here,' Dixon cut in. 'You'll smash the place up! Take your argument outside.'

'That suits me,' Chris Egan grated. 'Get moving, Deacon.'

'I'll stand my ground. This is as good a place as any,' Jeff responded, his right hand down at his side. 'The shooting started earlier, so it is open season now. Start the play any time you like.'

Chris Egan moved sideways a couple

of swift paces to clear the bar, his right hand sliding to his holstered gun. The man with him moved off to the right, putting distance between himself and the fat saloon owner. Jeff waited until Chris Egan began to draw his pistol before setting his hand in motion. He drew his Colt easily, cocked the weapon as it cleared leather, and his right index finger found the trigger with practised ease. The gun exploded, its detonation rattling bottles and glasses on the bar. The bullet took Chris Egan in the chest and he twisted away, dropping his half-drawn gun before slumping backwards to the floor.

The man with Egan had only begun to reach for his gun when Egan fell, and he hesitated, and then raised his hands.

'It ain't my fight,' he called. 'I'm not in this.'

Dixon was standing unmoving by the bar, both his hands in plain view, and he didn't even blink as he looked at Jeff's smoking gun. The tender stood frozen, both his hands out of sight behind the bar, his thin face set in a grimace of shock.

'You'd better put your hands where I can see them,' Jeff rasped, and Sowerby lifted his hands hastily and placed them palms down on the polished bar top. 'Now you'd better get rid of your gun in case you are tempted into making a fool play,' Jeff added.

Chris Egan's sidekick disarmed himself slowly, and his pistol thudded on the floor.

'I'm leaving now,' Jeff said. 'Nobody moves until you hear me riding away. OK?'

He stepped backwards towards the batwings, and halted quickly when a gun muzzle prodded his spine.

'You ain't going anywhere but jail,' Dan Ramsey's harsh voice said in his ear. 'Drop your gun, Deacon, or I'll split your backbone.'

'Well, look what's come out of the woodwork,' Jeff said harshly. 'I didn't start this play, Ramsey. That's Chris Egan, the bank robber, down on the floor, and he drew first. Ask Dixon what happened if you don't believe me. He saw the whole thing.'

'What about it, Dixon?' Ramsey demanded. 'What did you see?'

'I was talking to Egan when Deacon came in for a beer,' Dixon said reluctantly. 'Egan braced him, and made a play for his gun. Deacon beat him to it and shot him. It was self defence all right.'

'I want to put Deacon behind bars,' Ramsey said, 'so change your story, Dixon. What did you see?'

'Deacon came in looking for trouble,' Dixon said instantly, grinning. 'He drew his gun as soon as he saw Chris Egan, and shot him without giving him a chance. If Egan dies it will be cold-blooded murder.'

'That's better.' Ramsey grinned. 'You and Sowerby get your stories right and stick to them when Deacon stands trial. Now, do you wanta resist arrest, Deacon? I'd like nothing better than to plug you.'

'You're a lowdown four-flusher!' Jeff exclaimed. 'So you're coming out on the side of the Egans. That's no surprise, I guess. But you don't get me that easy.' He opened his fingers and his pistol thudded on the floor. 'Seeing that you're wearing a law badge I got no choice but to go quietly. I'll tell my side of the story to the sheriff.'

'Hell, I thought you'd go down fighting!' Ramsey slammed his gun barrel against the back of Jeff's head.

Jeff felt as if the saloon had fallen in on him. He dropped to his knees and then fell forward on to his face and remained motionless.

'I've been waiting a long time to do something about the Deacons,' Ramsey said, picking up Jeff's discarded gun. 'Now I've taken over from the sheriff you'd better play along with me, Dixon, or you'll be outa business before you can blink. Have you got that straight?'

'Anything you say, Dan,' Dixon replied without hesitation. 'I know which side my bread is buttered. I just hope you know what you are doing.'

'I know. Now you better get the doc in here to check out Egan. I'll put Deacon behind bars.' He motioned to the gunman accompanying Chris Egan. 'What's your name, mister?'

'Jack Arlot,' the man replied.

'OK, Arlot. Pick up your gun and give me a hand with Deacon. I want him behind bars. Did you see what happened when Deacon walked into the saloon?'

'Sure I did.' Arlot smiled. 'It was like Dixon said. Deacon didn't give Chris a chance.'

'So I got three witnesses who saw the same thing.' Ramsey holstered his gun and bent to grasp Jeff's shoulders. 'With three of you on my side I shouldn't have any trouble putting a rope around Deacon's neck when the time comes. Grab his legs and we'll tote him out of here.'

Dixon watched intently until Jeff was carried out to the sidewalk. When the batwings closed behind the deputy,

Sowerby shook his head.

'You know we can't go along with Ramsey, boss,' he said sharply. 'We can't stand by and watch Deacon hang if Egan dies.'

'So what do you suggest?' Dixon demanded. 'Ramsey is dangerous, like a mad bull, and I don't reckon to get on the wrong side of him. We have to go along with him, Al. He's been talking for some time about taking over from Kett, and it sounds like he's finally done it. Don't worry about Deacon. If he doesn't hang, the Egans will shoot him, so what's your beef? I reckon he'd rather be shot than die with a rope around his neck.'

'I don't wanta get mixed up in anything like lying a man's life away,' Sowerby protested.

'You are mixed up in it,' Dixon pointed out. 'But go ahead and tell Ramsey he's wrong, that you won't lie for him, and see what happens to you. Why the hell do you think I changed my story? Go up against Ramsey and he'll have us both hanging out to dry. You hold on here for the doc, and when he's finished lock up and go home. And you better think long and hard about what you're gonna say in your statement when Ramsey calls on you for one. Get it wrong and your light will go out pretty damn quick. I ain't joking. You better buck up your ideas because bar tenders are hard to find around here.'

Sowerby grimaced and helped himself to a drink. He watched Dixon leave the saloon, and his sour expression showed the grim direction of his thoughts.

Jeff was locked in a cell when he regained his senses. A single lantern cast a feeble yellow light which failed to reach the corners of the cell block. He was alone, and heavy silence pressed in around him. He sat up on the bunk on which he had been dumped and probed the back of his skull where Ramsey's gun barrel had caught him. He discovered a large bruise which filled his head with a painful throbbing, and closed his eyes to sit motionless for long moments, waiting for spasms of nausea to pass. When he felt easier he got to his feet and went to the barred door of the cell.

There was no reply from the front office when he shouted for the sheriff, and he waited an interminable time in the hope that someone would come to check on him. At length he returned to the bunk to review the situation, and soon realized what a mess he was in. He had been foolish to come back to town alone; he had played right into the hands of his enemies, and they would not miss an opportunity to put him out of the fight permanently. He wondered if Chris Egan was dead as he stretched out on the bunk and closed his eyes, grimly determined to escape at the first opportunity.

He drowsed, a hand to his aching head, but sleep eluded him and he felt as if the walls of the jail were closing in on him. He staggered when he pushed himself off the bunk, and fell against the cell door, grabbing at it for support. When the door pulled open he froze, contemplating the fact. Had Ramsey forgotten to lock it? He didn't think so as he stepped out of the cell and went to the door between the cells and the office and tried it carefully. It was locked. He looked around. There was a back door at the end of a short passage and he approached it, hoping against hope, and when it pulled open at his touch he stood motionless with the door ajar.

It had to be a gun trap, he thought. Ramsey would be outside in the shadows waiting for him with a gun. Jeff considered his chances. He had left his horse on the back lot behind the jail, and his rifle was in the saddle scabbard. He had about twenty yards to cover, and had no idea if Ramsey was alone out there or had recruited help to spring his trap. But he knew he could not stay bottled up in the jail. He had no choice but to make a run for it.

He eased the door to, went to the lamp on the wall and extinguished it, then returned to the door. A welcoming breeze blew into his face when he opened it slightly. He drew a deep breath and braced himself, then flung the door wide and dashed out into the alley and headed for the back lot like a rabbit running from a hungry coyote. A gun blasted the silence behind him and a slug snarled past his right shoulder. He flung himself down in the alley and scrambled along the ground to the rear corner of the jail. Bullets crackled around his fast moving figure, and he felt the burn of a slug across the outer side his left thigh just above the knee. He threw himself around the corner, lunged to his feet, and ran to where he had left his horse.

His breath was rasping in his throat when he spotted the animal. He ran to it, intent on getting his rifle. A pistol fired at him from the alley beside the jail and he ducked flying lead and grabbed at the reins as his horse cavorted nervously. He dragged his Winchester out of its scabbard and turned to face the alley, working the mechanism of the long gun with practised ease. Orange gun flashes stabbed through the shadows like probing fingers of fire, and he felt his Stetson jerk as a slug tore through its brim. He fired in return, sending three slugs into the alley mouth, and the shooting cut out, leaving sullen echoes grumbling away through the night.

Jeff grabbed his reins, swung into leather, and sent the horse off recklessly across the back lot. Behind him, the pistol resumed firing. He hunched low in his saddle, his rifle clutched in his left hand, and concentrated on getting speed from the nervous horse. He reached the livery barn, galloped around it, and headed along the trail for home range . . .

Dan Ramsey grinned in the darkness of the alley beside the jail as he reloaded his empty pistol with cartridges from the loops in his belt. So

Deacon had got away for the moment. That did not matter a hoot. He could hunt the man down at his leisure, and shoot him on sight because he was a fugitive from the law, and if Chris Egan died then so much the better because Deacon would be an escaped killer.

He went back to the street and entered the law office. Sheriff Kett was seated at his desk, and eyed Ramsey curiously.

'What was that shooting, Dan?' Kett demanded.

'That was Deacon making a break. I'll get after him in the morning. Right now I wanta check on Chris Egan.'

'You know Egan is wanted for bank robbery and murder, don't you?'

'He's kept his nose clean around here,' Ramsey replied. 'Anyway, if he's dead we can claim the reward on him. Leave it to me. I'll handle it.'

'You can't hunt Deacon down for killing an outlaw,' Kett observed. 'I'm not gonna get mixed up in anything like that. I'm quitting. You can have my job.

You've been after it long enough, and I've had my fill.'

'When are you pulling out?' Ramsey asked.

Kett sighed heavily and stood up. 'I'm going home right now. I'll ride out at sunup.'

Ramsey shook his head, his thoughts on the situation he had created. He realized that the sheriff had spoken the truth — he could not nail Jeff Deacon for shooting an outlaw. He would need a better reason to raise a hue and cry. Kett brushed past him on his way to the door, and Ramsey acted instinctively as his cunning mind thrust up a way of framing Jeff. He threw his left arm around the sheriff's neck and closed his fingers over the old lawman's mouth as he reached for the knife he carried in a sheath on his belt. He drove the blade into the sheriff's right side, just above the hip, and struck twice more while holding Kett motionless, thrusting the knife into the sheriff's stomach and chest.

Kett made no sound. Ramsey stretched the sheriff out on the floor, wiped his blade on Kett's shirt, and returned the weapon to its sheath. He left the office and locked the door. Jeff Deacon was wanted now as a sheriff killer.

5

Halloran stood at a front corner of the barn in the yard of the Deacon ranch and gazed out across the darkened range. He carried his rifle in his right hand; his ears strained for the slightest unnatural sound, and he was hair-triggered for trouble. The night breeze moaned around the barn, rattling a loose board in passing, but he was satisfied that nothing stirred out there in the dense shadows. He turned slowly, his gaze probing the darkness before he moved away from the barn and walked to the bunk house on the right. A harsh whisper came out of the shadows surrounding the low building, calling a challenge, and he halted before replying.

'I'm Clint Halloran,' he said, 'Jeff Deacon's pard. Jeff has ridden out for a spell and I'm keeping an eye open until he returns. Who are you?'

'Chuck Abelson, one of the crew. There are five of us and we are taking it in turns to watch for trouble. Those Egans are mighty tricky.'

'I saw some of them in town,' Halloran replied. 'You'd better be ready for them. They sure looked primed for trouble.'

'We're ready. You watch the far side of the yard and we'll cover this area.'

'Sure.' Halloran turned and made his way back to the barn.

As he eased back into the shadows the kitchen door of the ranch house closed with a thud, and he turned to inspect the shadows in that direction. A figure detached itself from the darkness of the house and came noiselessly across to the barn. He bent at the knees in order to silhouette the figure against the starry sky and recognized Tilda Deacon. She came within three feet of him and was not aware of his presence until he spoke. When he challenged her she halted in mid-stride in shock.

'Who's there?' she demanded.

'Halloran,' he replied.

She paused before him. 'I thought you had ridden out with Jeff.'

'He asked me to stick around and watch the place. What are you doing out here?'

'I figure to ride back to town. I want to see how Mack Egan is.'

'It's not safe for you to be out on the range alone,' he reproved. 'Why don't you wait until your family ride in tomorrow?'

She shook her head, and Halloran admired her spirit. 'Pa wouldn't let me see Mack; not in a thousand years,' she said in a low tone. 'I've got to go into town tonight.'

Halloran noted the stubborn tone in her voice and shook his head. 'I can't let you ride out alone,' he said firmly. 'It ain't fitting for you to travel alone.'

'Then come with me,' Tilda said instantly. 'I'm going if you like it or not.'

'Why make a difficult time much

worse by being unreasonable?' he countered. 'OK, so you hanker after Mack Egan, but your family have got their backs to the wall and it sure looks like the Egans figure to shoot them out of existence. Are you gonna run the risk of being taken by the Egans and held against the rest of the Deacons?'

'All I want to do is check on Mack,' she said stubbornly. 'If he is all right then I'll come right back here.'

'Sure, but if the Egans pick you up between here and town then there will be the devil to pay. You're not leaving, Tilda, so go on back into the house and wait for tomorrow. Mack Egan will keep. His life ain't in any danger.'

Tilda muttered and turned away. Halloran followed her back to the house and watched until she had entered. He heard the bar on the inside of the door drop into place and turned away to make a circuit of the barn. He was standing at a rear corner when he caught the sound of hoofs in the distance. Listening intently, he estimated at least six horses were on the move, and tightened his grip on the Winchester.

The riders were not approaching the house, Halloran discovered. He listened intently to their progress from west to east across the valley although they were too distant to be seen. He wondered who they were and what were they up to as he hurried around the barn to the bunkhouse.

'Abelson, did you hear those riders?' he called.

'Yeah, I got them pegged. Mitchell and Saunders are saddling up. They are gonna take a look-see to the south. I reckon the Egans are out for our herd, unless they want to draw us away before they attack the house.'

'I'll ride with your two men if the rest of you will cover the house,' Halloran decided.

Abelson emerged from the shadows around the bunkhouse. He was tall and thin, and starlight shone dully on the rifle in his hands.

'I'll introduce you to Mitchell. He's a good man. Don't take any chances if it is the Egans out there.'

Halloran followed the cowpoke across to the corral where two men were saddling up.

'Hey, Mitchell, this is Halloran, Jeff's pard,' Abelson said. 'He'll ride out with you.'

'Howdy?' Mitchell was big, wide-shouldered, and the hand he extended in greeting had a firm grip. 'Jeff has told us a lot about you, Halloran. Glad you are here. It looks like the Egans are on the move at last. Where is Jeff?'

'He rode out alone earlier.' Halloran borrowed Mitchell's rope, climbed into the corral, and tossed the loop over the head of his horse. He saddled up quickly, and Mitchell led the way across the yard.

'What's going on?' A voice called from the shadows on the porch.

'Is that you, Ham?' Mitchell replied. 'We heard riders so we're gonna check them out. You stay close to the house

102

and keep an eye on things, huh?'

'Sure thing,' Ham replied. 'It could be an Egan trick to draw some of you away from here. Watch your step. Who is riding with you?'

'Saunders, and Jeff's pard Halloran.'

'Don't let anything happen to Halloran,' Ham advised, and Halloran smiled as they continued out of the yard.

'We reckon there are six riders,' Mitchell said as they headed south. 'There's been some night riding through the valley. But we hadn't been attacked until earlier. I heard you and Jeff had some gun trouble in town.'

Halloran explained the events which had taken place. His eyes were fixed on the range ahead and his ears were strained for the sounds of horses moving. The valley was too quiet, he told himself. Half a dozen riders were out but there was no sign of them.

'They are south of us,' Saunders said in a grating tone. He had remained silent until now, and wheeled his horse to face the direction from which the sound had come originally.

They reined in and listened intently. Halloran heard a regular metallic sound which echoed eerily through the darkness.

'What in hell is that?' Saunders demanded.

'It sounds like someone banging a can with a pistol barrel,' Mitchell said. 'Sounds travel a heck of a long way in the night. Perhaps they heard us moving and are trying to trick us.'

'They'll have to do better than that,' Halloran said. 'Why don't you two ride back to the ranch and keep watch back there? I'll go on and take a look around, and it would be better if I do so alone.'

'You could get into a lot of trouble out here alone,' Mitchell observed.

'I'll take that chance,' Halloran replied.

'OK. Come on, Saunders. Let's head back to the ranch. Watch your step, Halloran.' Mitchell reined about without hesitation.

Halloran watched them ride off into

the night. When the sound of their hoofs had faded he returned his attention to the unknown riders but was still unable to hear them. He dismounted and led his horse in the direction he had heard the rapping sound. Moments later he picked up the sound of hoofs moving through the night, swung back into his saddle, and followed with his rifle ready in his left hand.

He continued, led on by the sound of hoofs thudding on the range. When he heard the bellowing of a steer he began to get an inkling of what was happening. The riders were about to run off the Deacon herd. He pushed his horse into a canter, thrust his rifle back into its scabbard, and drew his pistol. He heard the sound of cattle on the move and the riders began shouting encouragement to the stock.

Halloran topped a rise and reined in to peer across the shadowed range. A crescent moon was emerging from behind a distant peak, enabling him to see a sizeable herd of cattle being chivvied south. Half a dozen riders had to work hard to push the steers off home range because cattle were reluctant to move at night. Halloran touched spurs to his horse and moved down a slope towards the bawling mass, riding to converge on the nearest of the two drag riders.

Considerable noise and dust emanated from the herd when it got into its stride. Halloran pulled his neckerchief up over his nose and mouth as he approached at a canter. He stalked the nearest drag rider, closing in relentlessly, and was within a couple of yards before the drover saw him. The rustler reached for his holstered pistol. Halloran cocked his gun as he spurred his horse and sent the animal lunging in close.

'Drop the gun,' Halloran rasped.

The rustler paused with his pistol half-drawn. He found himself staring into the muzzle of Halloran's deadly weapon and promptly got rid of his

Colt. Halloran reached out with his left hand and seized hold of the rustler's reins. He struck at the man's head with his pistol barrel, and then struck again. The man pitched out of his saddle and Halloran dismounted and bent over him.

'Who are you?' Halloran demanded, thrusting the muzzle of his gun against the man's neck.

The rustler was dazed and shocked. He looked up at Halloran, shaking his head as he struggled to fully regain his senses.

'Where did you spring from?' he demanded in a dazed tone. 'I didn't see you coming.'

'Never mind that,' Halloran snapped. 'Tell me who you are and what you are doing here.'

'I'm Jake Tovey. I ride for Frank Egan. We're running off the Deacon herd.'

'That's all I need to know.' Halloran pushed off Tovey's Stetson and struck again with his pistol. Tovey groaned and fell back, senseless. Halloran used the man's lariat to hogtie him, and then swung back into his saddle and went on after the herd. He approached from the rear and found the second drag rider looking around for his companion.

'Where you been, Jake?' the rider called through the dust.

Halloran rode in close, his pistol cocked.

'Say, you ain't Jake!' the rustler ejaculated when Halloran was crowding him. He lifted his gun and Halloran fired. The bullet struck the rustler in the centre of the chest and he fell off his horse.

The shot echoed across the valley, setting the herd into a run that quickly turned into a stampede. Fear-maddened, the steers ran blindly despite the efforts of the remaining rustlers to control them. Guns hammered as the riders tried to turn the herd. Halloran spurred his mount and rode after them. The dust was much thicker. He rode along the right-hand side of the running cattle until he saw a rider ahead. The man was watching his back, and started shooting without warning. Slugs crackled around Halloran; he ignored the hostility, threw down on the rider, and squeezed off a shot. The man jerked and fell off his horse. Halloran galloped on, heading for the lead steers. He heard guns banging; he could see flashes where the rustlers were trying to stop the headlong flight of the steers, and headed for them, determined to wipe them out before they succeeded in regaining control.

The three surviving rustlers fled when Halloran started shooting in earnest, but another vacated his saddle before he could escape. Halloran reined in his horse, gazing around. He was alone now and he peered into the shadows. Dust was drifting thickly. The sound of pounding hoofs was receding: he was aware that he could not stop the stampede unaided. He went on, cantering behind the herd to ensure that the rustlers did not return, and at length the tired animals slowed and then halted their headlong rush. He rode slowly around them, well pleased with his efforts.

The herd settled down and Halloran moved fifty yards to the south and sat his horse, listening intently for sound. He expected the rustlers to return and kept his hand close to his pistol. The breeze blew into his face. He wondered about Jeff, aware that he should have accompanied his pard, but he could not be in two places at once and knew he had to stick with the cattle. When he heard horses approaching from the direction of the Deacon ranch he swung around and covered the four riders who came up.

'Over here,' Halloran called, cocking his gun, and the riders approached slowly. Mitchell was leading them, and the cowpoke reined in, his features pale in the moonlight.

'We heard the shooting and Ham told us to come and help you out, but it sure looks like you didn't need us,' Mitchell said.

'I got lucky,' Halloran replied. 'Push these steers back towards the ranch, huh? It ain't my line of work. I've got a prisoner back there and I'll pick him up. There are a couple of rustlers down, but they'll keep until sunup. Watch out for more trouble.'

'I don't think the Egans will come back for more of the same,' Mitchell responded. 'You sure gave them a bloody nose.'

Halloran rode back along the tracks of the herd and came upon Jake Tovey struggling to escape from his bonds. The rustler's horse was standing nearby with trailing reins. Halloran untied Tovey and took him along to the Deacon ranch. He rode into the front yard and Ham Deacon challenged him from the shadows around the porch.

'I wish I'd been with you,' Ham declared when Halloran told him what had occurred. 'It's a pity you didn't get all of them.'

'Four out of six is pretty good,' Halloran observed. 'We've got a prisoner as proof of who was responsible for the raid, and your crew are bringing the herd back.'

A figure approached from across the yard, and Abelson joined them.

'Ham,' the cowpoke said. 'Tilda just rode out. I tried to talk her out of riding at night but she wouldn't listen. She headed towards town. I thought you'd better know about it although she asked me not to tell.'

'You did right,' Ham replied. 'She's been moaning all evening about getting back to Mack Egan. It's a pity you didn't kill him when you had the chance, Halloran. Where has Jeff gone? Do you know?'

Halloran shook his head. 'I've got a hunch he was figuring on raising a little hell with the Egans at their place because they were here earlier, but I couldn't be sure. But in this situation, we must hit the Egans hard. It might make them have second thoughts about fighting.'

'His place is here,' Ham said

unhappily. 'I don't know what to do for the best. What would you do if you were in my boots, Halloran?'

'Exactly what you are doing,' Halloran replied. 'Your ranch is the most important place. Keep the Egans out of here and you've got a chance of beating them. So stick with it, Ham. I'll ride after Tilda if you'd like me to, and make sure she doesn't get into any trouble.'

'Thanks. It would ease my mind if you'd do that. I'd better tell Pa what has happened. I don't think we should ride into town tomorrow. The Egans might expect us to do that and show up here to burn the place while we are away. If you do see Jeff, ask him to split the breeze in this direction. I need help fast.'

'You're doing all right,' Halloran said, and swung into his saddle. He rode across the yard and set out for town, riding at a canter.

The herd was trailing back to the home pasture. Halloran reined in to talk to the cowpokes.

'Yeah, Tilda went past us like a bat outa hell,' Mitchell said in reply to Halloran's question. 'She damn near got herself shot, not stopping when we challenged her, and she kept right on going, heading for town. She shouldn't oughta be out alone after dark, huh?'

'She knows all about that,' Halloran replied. 'I'm on my way to watch she doesn't get into any trouble.'

He went on, and reached town without further incident. It was past midnight and nothing moved around the main street. Halloran looked for a saddle horse but none of the hitching rails he could see was in use. He rode along the street, looking left and right, wanting to check the doctor's place first. He saw a lighted window on the right, and when he reined up before it he spotted a brass name-plate on the wall beside the door.

Halloran dismounted and peered through the lighted window. Doc Woollard was bent over a figure lying on a table, his hands bloodstained and busy on his patient's chest. Halloran tapped on the window and Woollard looked up quickly. The doctor jerked his head, inviting Halloran in, and Halloran went to the door, found it unlocked and entered. He walked into the office and Woollard straightened. Halloran was shocked when he recognized the patient as Sheriff Kett.

'What happened to him?' Halloran demanded.

'He's been stabbed,' the doctor replied. 'And Ramsey, the deputy, has got half a dozen men together and set off to hunt down your pard Jeff Deacon; the word is that Jeff attacked the sheriff. It seems Jeff was jailed earlier for shooting Chris Egan, a known bank robber, but escaped from his cell. Ramsey tried to stop Jeff but failed, and found the sheriff in the law office, bleeding like a stuck pig.'

'Jeff wouldn't knife the sheriff,' Halloran said sharply. 'How is Kett? Will he live?'

'I don't think so.' Miller shook his

head. 'He's lost a lot of blood. He hasn't regained consciousness, and I don't think he will. He's just slipping away. One knife wound would have been more than he could stand, but whoever stabbed him was in a frenzy doing it.'

'What happened to Mack Egan after you patched him up?' Halloran asked.

'He's in the shack where he was shot. He'll be OK. What are you doing in town now? Has something happened in the valley?'

Halloran explained and the doctor shook his head. Halloran departed and led his horse to the far end of the street where the shacks and shanties were huddled together. He found Tilda's horse standing outside the Egan shack. There was a light in the window, and Halloran rapped on the door. When there was no reply he went to the window and peered inside. Mack Egan was sitting slumped on a chair at the table and Tilda was standing over him. Halloran rapped on the window and

116

Egan, turning quickly, lifted a pistol into view.

'You don't need a gun,' Halloran called, and went to the door, which was locked.

Tilda lifted the bar and opened the door. Halloran entered and came under the menace of Mack Egan's pistol.

'Put that away,' Halloran said. 'I'm not here to fight. Have you heard Sheriff Kett has been stabbed and is on the point of death? The doc said Ramsey took out a posse and is looking for Jeff. It seems Jeff was arrested for shooting Chris Egan but escaped from jail, and the sheriff was stabbed at that time.'

Mack Egan shook his head and Tilda groaned in disbelief.

'Jeff wouldn't knife the sheriff!' she gasped.

'Someone did,' Halloran mused. 'And I'm wondering where Jeff is right now. I'm certain he didn't stab the sheriff, so who did?'

'Do you think it was one of the

Egans?' Mack demanded.

'I don't make guesses,' Halloran replied. 'I've come to take you home, Tilda. I said it is too dangerous for you to be out alone, and I've had to leave the ranch to come for you. Anything could happen out in the valley while I'm not there, and Jeff is off riding someplace else. It would be a great time for the Egans to start shooting. They tried to run off the Deacon herd earlier but we stopped them.'

'Is Chris Egan dead?' Mack asked. He had lowered his pistol but held it ready for action.

'No.' Halloran shook his head. 'Jeff winged him. Chris is the one that brought in all the strangers, didn't he? Where does he fit into the Egan family?'

'Those strangers are his gang of robbers.' Mack shook his head. 'Chris is the black sheep of the family. He's my uncle — Burt's son, and he's been pushing the rest of the Egans into fighting the Deacons.'

'I need to get back to the valley,' Halloran said impatiently, 'and I'm not leaving without you, Tilda, so come along. You can see Mack is OK, and you can visit him again. Have some thought for your own family. If we don't stop this trouble there will be wholesale bloodshed.'

'Do like he says, Tilda,' Mack urged. 'He's got the rights of it. If one of your folks is killed by my family then we'll never be able to get together. Go on home, and I'll ride out to Bar E and see what I can do to put a stop to the trouble.'

Tilda gazed at Halloran while she considered the situation, and then she nodded.

'I'll ride back to the ranch with you.' She sighed. 'Have you any idea where Jeff is? If Dan Ramsey catches up with him then he'll be in bad trouble. Ramsey is a bully, and he's hoping to marry Mattie Egan. He'll do anything to get in good with the Egans. And he's been mighty thick with Chris Egan.'

'That's the plain truth of it,' Mack said, shaking his head. 'Ramsey is always out at our place, hanging around Mattie, and I've heard the way he talks about taking over from Sheriff Kett. If you made a list of the men who want the sheriff out of the way then Ramsey would have to be at the top. I don't know how he ever became a deputy. He is worse than anyone who has seen the inside of a jail. Uncle Chris said he knew Ramsey in Abilene a couple of years back, and at that time Ramsey was being hunted by the local law for robbery with violence. He'd made quite a name for himself, so Chris said.'

'And he is here now, working as a deputy?' Tilda was shocked. 'We've got to find Jeff before Ramsey can get to him, or stop Ramsey in his tracks,' she said grimly.

'Jeff may be back at the ranch now,' Halloran observed. 'He got out of jail and obviously left town. Knowing him, I'd say he went home.'

Tilda turned to the door, impatient

now to be on her way, and Halloran followed her, leaving Mack Egan gazing after them.

Halloran was tense on the ride back to Big D. If he had been in control of this fight from the start he would have stood in the Egan front yard throwing lead at the troublemakers until they were all dead, but it was not his fight, although he would side with Jeff all the way. He watched his surroundings closely as they rode, and was thankful that Tilda was not given to conversation. They rode in silence with only the creaking of saddle leather and thudding hoofs to accompany them.

He loosened his pistol in his holster when they had to cross the Egan range. The sky was bright with moonlight, but dense shadows occupied low ground and the blackness of the rim thrown across the valley by the moon seemed impenetrable. Halloran became hair-triggered, but even so he was startled when a gun flash split the darkness off to the left. Tilda uttered a cry and fell

121

out of her saddle. Halloran palmed his gun. By bending low over his saddle horn he was able to pick up movement, and made out the figures of two riders heading away across the range.

Halloran fired without seeming to aim. He closed his eyes to protect his night vision as the gun flashed, and when he opened them again he saw that one of the riders was down. The other vanished into the gloom and the sound of receding hoof beats faded into nothing. Halloran dismounted and hurried to Tilda's side. The girl was lying on her back. Halloran thought she was dead but she groaned when he moved her, and he could make out a dark stain of blood on her right shoulder.

'Are you hit bad, Tilda?' he demanded.

The girl groaned. She was only semi-conscious. Halloran glanced around, decided there was no further danger, and struck a match to examine her. He discovered that she had been hit high in the shoulder and was losing blood. He used his neckerchief to bind the wound and then lifted her back into the saddle, ignoring her protests. His mind was attuned to attacking the Egans as he continued to the Deacon ranch . . .

Jeff, when he left town, headed for Sunset Valley by the shortest route, making a bee-line across the range. He was shocked by Dan Ramsey's gun trap back in town and promised himself a reckoning with the tough deputy. He figured it was bad enough having to fight the Egans without the law taking sides, and Sheriff Kett had shown sympathy for the Egans despite the fact that none of the Deacons had ever put a foot wrong where the law was concerned.

He reached the crossing where the trail continued on the Egan range and reined in to check for riders. It was a favourite hold-up spot for the Egan crew and Jeff was not in the mood for any more trouble. He was tempted to ride to the Egan house and shoot up the place but quashed the impulse:

there was enough trouble ahead without stirring up the Egans.

The sound of several horses on his back trail alerted him to danger and he rode into cover and dismounted. Minutes later five riders showed up and reined in close to where he had halted. Dan Ramsey's harsh voice broke the silence, and Jeff, as he listened to the deputy's voice, promised himself an early reckoning with the bullying lawman.

'OK, men,' Ramsey said. 'You go on to Big D and look around for Jeff Deacon. I'm gonna ride on to the Egan spread and acquaint them with the news of what's happened in town. They'll be interested to hear that Jeff Deacon knifed the sheriff. If you don't find him at Big D I'll have every able-bodied man in the county out tomorrow looking for him. Remember he's desperate, and he can handle a gun, so you'll have to shoot on sight if you come up with him.'

'The sheriff ain't dead yet,' someone

remarked. 'Doc said he might live.'

'I'm handling this as if Kett has already snuffed it,' Ramsey snarled. 'Don't take any chances with Deacon, you hear? Give him any kind of a chance and some of you will be biting the dust. He's a killer, and from what I've heard of him he ain't likely to take prisoners.'

Jeff frowned as he listened to the conversation. Joe Kett had been stabbed and was not expected to live! He watched the posse men ride off in the direction of Big D. Ramsey sat his horse for some moments, gazing after the riders, and then turned his mount and headed in the direction of Bar E. Jeff remained in cover, shocked by what he had overheard, and was at a loss about how to proceed. Who could have stabbed the sheriff? Ramsey had set a gun trap outside the jail with the intention of murdering him, but had the bullying deputy also knifed Kett?

There appeared to be no reason why Ramsey would want to kill the sheriff.

Jeff pushed his horse into movement and rode out of cover after the deputy. He needed some answers to the host of questions teeming through his mind, and Ramsey was the only man who had some or all of those answers.

Ramsey sent his horse at a lope across the range, his figure black in the night, and Jeff went after him openly, figuring that when Ramsey heard him the deputy would think it was one of his posse men chasing after him. Ramsey evidently heard hoof beats for he twisted in his saddle and looked back. He reined in and sat waiting for Jeff to reach him.

Jeff drew his pistol and covered Ramsey as he reined in. Ramsey leaned forward to peer at Jeff, and when he saw the levelled gun he lifted his hands.

'Deacon!' he observed. 'What the hell is this?'

'You set me up at the jail,' Jeff accused.

'Why did you knife Kett?' Ramsey countered.

'I didn't. I reckon you know more

126

about that than me.'

'All I know is that you escaped from jail, stabbing the sheriff in the process, and left him for dead in the office.'

'Is that the tale you're telling? I left the jail by the back door. I didn't go into the office. I know I didn't do it so I'm looking to you for some answers, Ramsey. I reckon you did for the sheriff and I wanta know why.'

'You're loco if you're gonna try and use that as an answer to the charge of murder.' Ramsey laughed. 'I got you dead to rights, Deacon. You were in the jail and you busted out. I found Kett lying on the floor of the office with knife wounds, and the doc said he ain't gonna pull through. That's all I needed to turn out the posse for you, and I'll see you with a rope around your neck for what you've done.'

'You won't get away with it.' Jeff snatched Ramsey's pistol from its holster and stuck it into his waistband. 'You're not gonna ride roughshod over me. I'll take you to Big D and hold you there until you come up with the truth. It is obvious you've thrown in with the Egans so I'll keep you out of circulation until I find out what happened in town earlier. I know I didn't knife the sheriff, so that leaves you, Ramsey.'

'If you had any sense you'd be splitting the breeze to other parts,' Ramsey said. 'You ain't got a chance. The law is behind me. No one is gonna take the word of a two-bit gunman against a deputy.'

'You're loco if you think you can get away with something like that. Come on, we're riding to Big D. You're finished as a deputy. I heard that you are wanted in Abilene for robbery with violence. I guess the law department there will be pleased to know your whereabouts, Ramsey, and don't even think of giving me any trouble because I'll shoot you like a dog if you try anything.'

Ramsey shook his reins, wheeled his mount, and then launched himself sideways at Jeff. His left hand grasped

Jeff's gun wrist and pushed the weapon aside. When his heavy body crashed against Jeff they both went over Jeff's horse and fell to the ground. Ramsey retained his hold on Jeff's wrist, forced the pistol upwards, and his right fist sledged against Jeff's jaw.

Jeff clenched his teeth as his senses swirled. He slammed his left fist into Ramsey's face. Ramsey yelled and jerked away, losing his hold on Jeff's gun. He scrabbled for a fresh grip on Jeff's wrist but Jeff struck fiercely with his gun barrel and laid the heavy metal against Ramsey's left temple. Ramsey slumped instantly. Jeff pushed himself away from the deputy and staggered to his feet. His senses were reeling from the blow he had received but he moved back out of reach and levelled his gun at Ramsey as the man staggered to his feet with every intention of continuing. But he pulled up sharply when he found himself looking into Jeff's gun muzzle.

Ramsey raised his hands, breathing heavily.

'Turn around,' Jeff rasped, and Ramsey did so reluctantly.

Jeff struck Ramsey again, slamming his gun barrel against the back of the deputy's skull. Ramsey folded without a sound and fell on his face. Jeff stood breathing deeply, watching the deputy for tricks, but Ramsey was out cold. Jeff holstered his gun and searched Ramsey's saddle bags. He found a pair of handcuffs and put them on Ramsey wrists, then boosted the deputy across his saddle and mounted his horse to head for the Big D by a circuitous route.

When Ramsey regained his senses he began to curse loudly. Jeff was watching his surroundings and listening intently for sounds, and threatened Ramsey to shut him up.

'Open your mouth again and I'll bend my gun barrel on your thick skull,' he vowed.

Ramsey lapsed into silence and they continued until the sound of approaching hoofs alerted Jeff. He reined in, turning his head slowly to pick up the direction from which the sounds were coming. Ramsey straightened in his saddle.

'Hey, you riders,' he called stridently. 'This is Dan Ramsey over here. Jeff Deacon has got me handcuffed. Come and get him.'

Jeff struck at Ramsey and the deputy slumped forward over his saddle horn but the approaching riders had been alerted. Jeff ducked as guns hammered, and he heard the crackle of closely passing slugs as he dropped the lead rope of the deputy's horse and spurred his mount away into the shadows. But he did not ride far. He halted and stepped down from the saddle, gun in hand. He could hear Ramsey's excited voice giving the newcomers his version of recent events.

Two riders had approached the deputy, and one of them spurred his horse to chase Jeff, who dropped to one knee and lifted his Colt. He got the man silhouetted against the sky but held his fire. Then he shouted a challenge, his voice echoing in the silence of the night. The rider fired instantly and his slug struck the ground only inches from Jeff's left knee. Jeff squeezed his trigger and the rider fell sideways off his horse.

The echoes of the shot grumbled away across the range. Jeff got to his feet and walked towards Ramsey and the second rider, aware that the shooting had started with a vengeance: there could be no hope of reconciliation between the Deacons and the Egans. Blood had been shed on both sides, and it would depend on gun speed and accuracy to put an end to the trouble. Jeff did not intend to be on the losing side. He walked towards Ramsey, who was shouting for a gun. The rider with Ramsey dismounted hurriedly. He began to fire indiscriminately at where he thought Jeff was waiting, and the night was rent by gun flame and thunder.

6

Halloran was relieved when he reached the Deacon spread. Tilda was slumped in her saddle, groaning intermittently, and he was concerned for her. A light in a downstairs window of the ranch house guided him to the yard, but he stopped short of the fence surrounding it when he caught a suspicious sound to his right. He palmed his gun and faced the sound. A patch of scrub was growing on a knoll and he covered it.

'OK,' he called, thinking a guard was concealed in the shadows. 'Come on out and identify yourself.'

'Don't shoot,' a female voice replied, and a slight figure armed with a rifle arose and came forward.

Halloran recognized Cora Deacon. The girl's face was pale and tense in the moonlight.

'What are you doing?' He demanded.

'Ham needed a spell because he's been out here for hours. Who is that with you?'

'It is Tilda, and she's been shot.'

Cora gasped and ran to her sister's side. 'What happened?' she demanded.

'We ran into trouble as we crossed the Egan range,' Halloran explained. 'She's not seriously hurt, but we'd better get her into the house and tend her. Then I'm gonna ride over to the Egan place and shoot a few holes in some of that brood. They need to be taught a lesson.'

'Have you seen Jeff anywhere?' Cora took the reins of Tilda's horse and led it across the yard to the house. Halloran followed, leading his mount, and hitched the animal to the rail in front of the porch.

He eased Tilda out of the saddle and carried her into the house. Ham and Asa Deacon were seated in the big room, and both men sprang up in shock. Halloran remained in the background while they examined Tilda.

Ham took up his rifle and went out to the porch, Halloran following him. They stood looking into the shadows, probing the darkness for signs of trouble.

'There's nothing for it,' Ham said at length. 'I'm gonna have to ride over to Bar E and shoot me a few Egans.'

'You'd better stay here and guard the spread until Jeff shows up,' Halloran advised. 'I'll deal with the Egans. It's about time we got in a few licks at them.'

'Do you know where the Egan ranch is?' Ham demanded.

'No, but you can spare a man to show me the way. I'll be back before sunup and the Egans won't be so keen to fight after I've put some of them down in the dust.'

'Maybe you'd better wait for Jeff to come back before you try something like that,' Ham said dubiously. 'You might trigger a full scale war in the valley which will swallow us up like a prairie fire. I sure wish Jeff was here to handle this. He had no right to ride off like he did. I don't know anything about fighting; I ain't ever left this ranch in ten years. Working cattle is all I know. Jeff was the fiddle-foot. He never could settle down in one spot. But I guess you know that, huh?'

'Sure. I sympathize with you, Ham, but you'd better stay put while I ride out.'

'I know you're right.' Ham shrugged. 'That's the hell of it!'

The front door opened and Cora appeared. She came to stand between Halloran and Ham.

'How is Tilda?' Ham demanded.

'She'll be OK in a few days.' There was no trace of sympathy in Cora's tone. 'Perhaps it will teach her to stay home when she's told.' She turned to Halloran, her face showing pale in the moonlight. 'Were you serious about riding over to the Egan spread and shooting the hell out of them?'

'That's what I've got in mind,' he said.

'Then I'll ride with you,' Cora spoke as if she would take no refusal. 'I can show you the way, and I'd sure like to start hitting back at the Egans.'

'No dice!' Halloran replied without hesitation. 'Stay here where you will be safe. I've wasted a good deal of time going after Tilda, and I don't want anything bad happening to you. I'll take Mitchell with me, if that's OK by you, Ham.'

'Whatever you say,' Ham agreed.

'Mitchell is needed here,' Cora said. 'You don't have to worry about me, Halloran. I can use a rifle as good as any man and I always hit what I aim at. I'll show you the way to the Egan place and toss a few slugs into them while I'm at it. It's about time we started hitting them where it hurts.'

'Wait here until Jeff gets back, and if he says you can go on the warpath then it'll be all right by me,' Halloran said. 'I'm definitely not dragging any female around. You could get yourself killed, and I wouldn't want you on my conscience.' He paused, and when Cora opened her mouth to continue her argument he cut her short. 'You're wasting your breath,' he rapped. 'Stay home and tend your sister.'

Cora gazed at him for a moment and then turned and went back into the house.

'It's about time someone made my sisters toe the line,' Ham said with a bitter laugh. 'But if Cora has made up her mind to ride with you then nothing short of a blue norther will stop her. I'll go tell Mitchell to ride out with you.'

Halloran remained on the porch watching the shadows, his ears strained for any sound. He was hoping Jeff would show up, but there was still no sign of his pard by the time Ham returned with Mitchell.

'Just show Halloran the way to the Egan spread and then come back here,' Ham instructed.

'I'd like a chance to shoot me an Egan,' Mitchell replied. 'I'd settle for

Buck or Ezra, or better yet, both of them.'

'You'll get your chance later,' Ham said. 'I need you here in case any of the Egans have the same idea as Halloran.'

Halloran rode out with Mitchell and they headed south-west across the darkened range. They did not talk and watched their surroundings carefully. Once, Mitchell called a halt because he thought he heard a suspicious sound, and they sat with their hands on their pistols, ready to draw and start shooting. But the night remained silent, and after some tense moments they rode on.

The moon was dropping behind the eastern horizon when Mitchell reined in just below the crest of a hogback ridge. The night was darker now and they gazed at each other in the dense shadows.

'The Egan place is just over this ridge,' Mitchell said. 'If they've got guards out then you'll have to be careful from here on in.'

'Thanks,' Halloran replied. 'You can leave me now. If you hear shooting just ignore it.'

'Give them some shots for me. Those bozos have been giving us a pretty hard time lately.' Mitchell turned away and rode into the shadows.

Halloran sat listening to the cowpoke's departure, and when full silence came he crossed the ridge and eased down off the skyline. He could discern the buildings of the Egan ranch, and rode slowly through cover until he reached level range. There he dismounted and walked his horse closer to the silent spread. He left the horse a couple of hundred yards out from the ranch yard, knee-hobbling the animal to keep it immobile. He drew his Winchester from its scabbard and checked his pistol before moving on foot to the yard itself. The silence of the range closed around him like a cloak.

He expected to find at least one guard watching the spread, and crouched in the shadows of the rail fence to check.

The silence was overwhelming. A faint breeze was blowing cool on the back of his neck. He listened intently but heard nothing, and was about to enter the yard when he caught sight of a flaring match over by the corral. He waited, watching for movement, and a lighted cigarette began to glow. By degrees he made out the indistinct figure of a man leaning against the rails of the corral.

Halloran began to stalk the man. He stayed in dense shadows and walked slowly around the yard until he reached the rear of the house, which he skirted. An open space existed between the house and the cook shack, and he kept the small building between the corral and himself as he edged closer. He moved around the shack and found himself only a dozen yards from the corral. The guard was still leaning on the corral, his cigarette glowing as he smoked.

Holding his rifle in his left hand, Halloran drew his pistol and stepped out towards the guard. He covered half the distance to the corral before the man heard a sound and turned quickly, his cigarette falling from his mouth in shock. Halloran saw him begin to lift the rifle he was holding, and called in a harsh undertone.

'Forget it, mister. I got you cold. Drop the gun or I'll drop you.'

The guard froze, and then opened his right hand and the rifle dropped into the dust.

'Get your hands up way above your shoulders,' Halloran commanded, 'and then turn your back to me.'

The man obeyed and Halloran went in close to relieve him of a holstered pistol.

'That's good,' Halloran commented. 'Now we'll take a walk around the corral. Do it as if you're scouting around. Get moving.'

The guard moved slowly, his hands high, and Halloran went with him, staying just out of arm's length. When they were out of sight of the house, Halloran called a halt.

'This will do,' Halloran said. 'What's your name, mister?'

'Bill Hankey. Who in hell are you, sneaking in here like this? You could have gotten yourself killed.'

'An army could have marched in here and you wouldn't have noticed,' Halloran said in grim amusement. 'Listen, I'll ask the questions and you stick to answering them. OK?'

'Sure. You're holding all the cards, mister.'

'How many men are on the spread?' Halloran continued.

'Counting the Egans, there must be fifteen at least. Are you planning to hold them all up?'

'Don't worry about my plans. Are there any women in the house?'

'Only Mattie Egan, Frank's daughter. She wouldn't leave. Frank cleared the other womenfolk out of here a couple of weeks ago. Did the Deacons send you here?'

'I'm just looking around,' Halloran replied. 'I've got some work to do. Are you the only guard?'

'There's only one ranch; so only one guard,' Hankey retorted.

'I'll come back and kill you if I find you're lying about anything,' Halloran warned.

'What are you gonna do with me?'

'Don't give me any trouble and I'll leave you hogtied behind a bush. It's your choice what happens to you.'

'I'll stay quiet,' the man decided.

Halloran escorted Hankey to the spot where he had left his horse. He opened a saddle-bag and took out a short length of rope using it to bind Hankey's hands and feet. He removed Hankey's neckerchief and gagged him with it and then issued a warning for Hankey to remain silent. He turned and retraced his steps to the yard, staying clear of the house, and then entered the barn cautiously.

There was straw in the loft and Halloran climbed a ladder and set fire to it. In seconds a conflagration flared and he beat a retreat back to ground level. By the time he reached the cook shack he could see flames darting up through the roof of the barn. He went back to the corral, opened the pole gate, and chased out a score of horses. As the animals crossed the yard he fired a couple of shots skywards to encourage them to keep running. With the echoes of the shots ringing out, he moved clear and waited in the shadows, able to see the doors of the bunk house and the ranch house. Behind the house a red glow grew rapidly as fire engulfed the barn.

A light appeared in the window of the bunk house. Halloran watched closely, and when the bunk house door began to open cautiously he used his Winchester to put three rapid shots into the woodwork. The door was suddenly jerked wide and a man staggered out into the open, reeling drunkenly before pitching forward on to his face. The light inside the bunk house was extinguished. Almost immediately a man's voice yelled from the shadows on the porch.

'What in hell is going on? Who fired those shots? Hankey, where are you?'

Halloran lifted his rifle to his shoulder and fired rapidly at the porch. He spread his shots across the broad front of the house and triggered the long gun until the magazine was empty. Drawing his pistol, he eased back from the ranch without incident. The night took on a ruddy hue as the barn burned. He did not look back but returned to his horse, reloaded his weapons, and rode out.

From the hogback ridge the burning barn looked like a fiery beacon. Halloran watched it for a few moments and then rode out for the Deacon spread, grimly satisfied with the result of his foray . . .

Jeff Deacon traded lead with the rider beside the helpless Ramsey. He could dimly hear Ramsey shouting for a gun but kept his attention fixed on the rider. Gun flashes erupted, puncturing the shadows as the man triggered his

Colt. Two slugs crackled past Jeff's head and he ducked and threw himself flat even as he returned fire. He squeezed his trigger and flame spurted from his muzzle. The rider jumped and then twisted and fell off his horse. Jeff got to one knee, eyes squinting against muzzle flame, and the hollow echoes of the shooting grumbled away across the range. An orange flash stabbed at him from the spot where the rider had gone down, and the next instant Jeff received a terrific blow in his left side. It was as though the night itself had exploded in his face. Pain stabbed through his body, but before he could accept that he had been shot the sky seemed to fall in on him and he pitched forward on his face and lay motionless.

Ramsey sprang from his saddle, watching the spot where Jeff had gone down. He moved to Jeff's side and picked up his gun. With his wrists handcuffed, Ramsey was awkward handling the pistol, but he cocked the gun. It was in him to shoot Jeff in cold blood, but he held his fire when he found Jeff unconscious. He dropped to one knee beside Jeff and searched him for the handcuffs key, which he found in a breast pocket. Unlocking the cuffs, he snapped them around Jeff's wrists and then examined Jeff to estimate the seriousness of his wound. He found a patch of blood over Jeff's left lower ribs and struck a match to take a closer look at his prisoner's condition.

'It looks like you'll live to hang,' Ramsey observed. He hauled Jeff to his feet and threw him across a saddle, then remounted and led Jeff's horse towards the Egan spread.

Jeff regained consciousness to find himself face down across a jolting saddle. He was dazed, shocked, and pain filled his body; aggravated by every movement of the horse. He tried to push himself off the saddle and realized his wrists were cuffed together. Ramsey saw Jeff's movement, cursed vehemently and then leaned sideways to strike at him with the barrel of his pistol. Jeff tried desperately to avoid the blow but failed, and his pain receded into blessed unconsciousness as the gun barrel rapped his skull.

Ramsey found the Bar E blazing with yellow lamplight when he reached the yard of the big ranch. There were several men standing on the porch before the open doorway of the house. He rode across the yard and men drew their guns and covered his approach. He heard the guns being cocked, and called out urgently.

'Hey, hold your fire, boys. It's Dan Ramsey coming in with a prisoner.'

Frank Egan came to the edge of the porch, his gun levelled at the two approaching riders.

'It's Ramsey OK,' he said at length. 'Who have you got there, Dan?'

'Someone you'll be mighty pleased to see,' Ramsey laughed. 'It's that two-bit gunman, Jeff Deacon. He killed the sheriff in town earlier tonight and I nailed him crossing your range.'

'He killed Joe Kett?' Frank Egan was

astonished by the news. 'What the hell happened?'

'I arrested Deacon for shooting Chris Egan in the big saloon in town.' Ramsey had his story of the events in Plainsville worked out to his satisfaction. 'Chris ain't hurt bad, and Mack is at your shack in town. Mack was shot accidently. But the sheriff was knifed several times when Deacon escaped from jail. There's gonna be hell to pay over this. But it looks like the game is going your way without a big fight, Frank. I sent a posse out to Big D, and with any luck there'll be shooting and some more of the Deacons will stop lead.'

'Is Deacon dead?' Frank Egan demanded.

'He's hit bad. I don't know if he'll die. If you want him you can have him, but if you don't I'll put him back in jail and, if he pulls through, charge him with killing the sheriff. He'll hang for sure.'

'Jail him,' Frank decided. 'With him

out of the way we can handle the rest of the Deacons.'

'I'll stay here tonight and ride on to town in the morning,' Ramsey decided. 'Your cook is good at doctoring so get him to check Deacon. I don't want him to die on me. I'll get a lot of pleasure from seeing him hang.'

Frank looked around at his companions, all Egans, and grinned. 'We'll ride out at first light,' he decided. 'In the morning we're gonna clear the Deacons out of the valley.'

'I'm ready to ride into Big D right now,' said Ezra, his eldest son.

'Tomorrow will do,' Frank replied. 'It's about time we wrapped up this business. Have one of the crew on guard through the night. They can arrange it between themselves. The rest of you better get some shuteye. It looks like being a busy day tomorrow. Come on in, Ramsey, I guess you'll wanta see Mattie. If Deacon is dripping blood then put him in the barn. Ezra, tell Cookie to patch him up, if he can. We'd sure like to see him live to hang, huh?'

Ramsey dismounted and stepped on to the porch. Two of Frank's sons lifted Jeff off his horse, carried him around the house to the barn and dumped him on a pile of straw. Ezra went for the cook. Jeff regained consciousness when the pain of the cook's rough ministrations stabbed through his shock.

'Take it easy, feller,' advised Bill Callan, the cook. 'It looks like you're slated to hang. They tell me you knifed Sheriff Kett.'

'No.' Jeff shook his head. 'I didn't do it. Where am I hit?'

'The bullet hit one of your lower ribs and was deflected outwards. If it had gone the other way you'd be dead now. Maybe it would have been better if you'd died from a slug instead of getting strung up for murder. Anyway, I've stopped the bleeding and you should be OK.'

Jeff closed his eyes. Pain was throbbing through his left side. The cook began to bandage his wound and his senses faded once more. Ezra Egan watched impassively.

'Get someone to watch him when you've finished, Bill,' he said at length 'I wouldn't want him to cheat the hangman.'

Callan bound Jeff's left arm to his chest to take pressure off the wound. He called in the guard and instructed him to keep an eye on Jeff. The guard stood in the doorway of the barn for some moments before crossing to Jeff's side. He toed Jeff in the ribs, and, when Jeff did not stir, turned and set off to make a round of the yard. Jeff was disturbed by the boot and opened his eyes. He stifled a groan when he tried to move. Pain was rampant in his side and chest. For some moments he could not recall what had occurred but his thoughts began to revolve and he gritted his teeth. He looked around for Ramsey, found the barn deserted, and forced himself to his knees.

His one thought was of escape — he needed to get away. If Ramsey jailed him for the murder of the sheriff he would be finished, because the bullying deputy would never release him. He got to his feet and stood swaying, waiting for a paroxysm of dizziness to pass. He leaned heavily against a post and looked around for a weapon.

He stood with his eyes closed, willing himself to find the strength to go on. When he was able to move he lurched to the back door of the barn and staggered out into the darkness. The cool night air did him a power of good and he moved through the darkness to the corral. There was a light in the cook shack and he paused to peer through a window to see the cook sitting at a table, supping from a whiskey bottle. He remained in the shadows, looking for the guard, and spotted the man across the yard, making a circuit of the perimeter of the ranch, rifle held ready as he checked the shadows.

Jeff looked in the corral and saw his own mount inside with a dozen other horses. He noticed a rope coiled on a post and picked it up, but with his left arm bound to his chest he knew he had little chance of roping the horse. He tossed the rope aside and went to the tack shed, picked up a bridle, and slipped between the bars of the corral. The horses became restive as he walked through them to his own mount. He called softly to the animal and it pricked up its ears, but moved off uneasily when he reached out to grasp its forelock.

The guard reached the barn and looked inside. Jeff heard him call out in alarm when he found his prisoner gone. The man emerged from the barn, shouting an alarm, and then came towards the corral. He banged on the cook shack window in passing.

'Hey, Cookie,' he called, 'the prisoner ain't in the barn. Have you seen him?'

There was no reply from the cook, and the guard reached the corral and looked over the horses. Jeff remained behind his own horse, and moved with it when it began to circle. The guard

155

climbed between the poles to take a closer look at the animals. He noticed their uneasiness and became suspicious. Jeff prepared to fight. When the guard reached the head of his horse he stepped around the animal and lunged at the man.

His clenched right hand delivered a blow to the guard's chin and the man uttered a low cry. He dropped to one knee and Jeff kicked him in the head. The guard dropped flat, losing his grip on his Winchester. Jeff snatched up the weapon. He checked the mechanism, jacked a shell into the breech, and steeled himself to go on. He heard a voice calling from the porch and looked around to see two figures coming towards the corral.

He slipped between the poles of the corral and exerted himself to continue. He needed to get clear, maybe lose himself in the night. He walked around the cook shack and moved away, keeping the shack between himself and the two men. His legs felt as if they did not belong to him. His knees were trembling and he walked like a drunken man, legs stiff and feet splayed. He managed to keep his balance, and started across the range in the direction of Big D, keeping a tight grip on the rifle. He was determined to sell his life dearly if the Egans found him.

Jeff covered two hundred yards before his legs let him down. He fell into the lush grass and lay unmoving for seemingly long minutes while his senses slipped into and out of unconsciousness. Sweat beaded his forehead and face and he could feel blood running from his wound. The pain was fierce, throbbing, and he rolled on to his back and looked up at the starry night sky. He was miles from the ranch and keenly aware that he could not walk that distance. He was safe at the moment, but when daylight came he would stand out like a sore thumb and the Egans would surely get him.

He used the rifle to prop himself up and gained his feet with a great effort.

His senses swam and tilted. The ground seemed to be moving alarmingly and he closed his eyes. His balance deserted him and he pitched on to his face again. His senses faded and he was filled with nausea. He lay unmoving, unaware of his situation for more than an hour before full consciousness returned. When he opened his eyes he was gazing up at the sky. He noted that the moon was in a different position from the last time he had seen it. The pain in his chest was constant, but he felt rested and made an effort to rise. He picked up the rifle, levered himself to his feet, and looked around to get his bearings.

Cold sweat stood out all over him when he lurched forward, driven by an animal instinct to survive. He felt weak as a kitten but forced himself to move with indomitable determination. He pushed his left leg forward and tottered as he fought to maintain his balance, using the rifle as a crutch, the muzzle digging into the grass as he leaned his weight on it. He paused before making the effort to take another step. His legs trembled and it was in him to give up, drop to the ground and lie on his face in blissful rest. But he forced himself to go on. He had to be away from Egan range before the sun came up or he would die when they came looking for him.

He made an almighty effort to control his movements and began to put one foot in front of the other with an irregular rhythm, concentrating on keeping to the direction he needed to find safety. He lost all track of time and longed to stop and rest, but to rest was to die and he kept moving.

The sound of distant shooting came to him and he paused to glance back the way he had come. Were the Egans out looking for him already? He heard a lot of shooting, but then it shut down and echoes faded. He went on again, nerving himself to keep his legs moving.

Later, when he heard hoof beats off to his left he dropped flat and listened intently to a rider moving past him at a fast pace, unaware that it was Halloran riding back to Big D after shooting up Bar E. He lifted the rifle but their trails did not cross and he listened to the horse going on towards Big D. He wondered about the shooting, but felt certain the rider was not an Egan, because no one would ride alone on a man hunt.

When full silence returned he continued, the torture of moving gripping him as he progressed. The moon disappeared beyond the horizon and the night grew imperceptibly darker. His strength was failing, and his thoughts stopped revolving in his head. All he could think about was to keep his legs moving, but suddenly he realized he was on all fours and crawling, and could not remember how long he had been off his feet.

He flopped on his face, and was wondering if he could summon up enough strength to rise when he heard riders coming from the direction of Bar

E. He sat up and checked the rifle. The Egans were coming at last, and he could not run. He had to make a stand. He waited stoically, his eyes unblinking as he stared into the shadows. He counted three horses approaching. They seemed to be travelling in the direction he was taking but he did not think they could be trailing him in the night. He prepared to fight because he had no alternative.

The riders loomed up out of the gloom, three of them cantering in the direction of Big D, and he knew they could only be Egans. He lifted the rifle, his teeth clenched against pain, and the riders were just twenty yards away when he challenged them.

'If you're Egans then start shooting!' he yelled.

The riders reined in quickly and then began to separate. One of them had fast reflexes because he started shooting almost before Jeff had finished speaking. Jeff heard a slug crackle past his head and fired in the same instant. The rider went out of his saddle but continued to shoot from a prone position. The other two split up quickly, one riding to the left and the other going to the right. Jeff sent a couple of shots after them, and then flattened out in the grass as a hail of lead came back at him.

Gun flashes slashed through the darkness and heavy echoes crashed across the range. Jeff kept low, hoping the magazine of the rifle was fully loaded. The chips were down and the fatal game of shoot-your-neighbour had started in earnest.

7

Halloran was well pleased as he returned to Big D. He had issued a declaration of war to the Egans and fully expected them to show up at the Deacon ranch to retaliate confident that in an open fight he could shoot the hell out of them. The even texture of the night sky was greying in the east as he rode into the Deacon yard. He reined in when a challenge came to him from the shadows around the house and, when he replied, Ham Deacon appeared with a rifle in his hands.

'Howdy, Ham. Has Jeff returned yet?'

'No, he ain't showed.' Ham's voice was filled with concern. 'I'm worried about him, Halloran. A posse showed up from town to arrest him for knifing Sheriff Kett. They reckoned Jeff did it.'

'I was at the doctor's house last night,' Halloran said. 'Doc doubted that

163

Kett would survive. I don't think Jeff did it. I reckon he's been set up.'

'That ain't what the posse told me. Dan Ramsey, the county deputy, was a witness, and there ain't a chance of arguing against him.'

'I wouldn't put any trust in anything Ramsey said,' Halloran observed. 'He's wanted for robbery with violence in Abilene. It is obvious he is sympathetic to the Egans, and it looks like framing Jeff is how he's trying to help them. Looking at it that way, I'd say Ramsey stabbed the sheriff and is laying the blame at Jeff's door.'

'Whatever way you look at it, Jeff is in a lot of trouble,' Ham said tensely. 'The posse men are good, solid citizens. They are not on one side or the other in this trouble, but they came in here prepared to shoot Jeff on sight. They are not gonna give him a chance, Halloran. They want him dead or alive, and one of them said Ramsey would prefer him dead. What I can't understand is why Jeff didn't come back here when he got out of jail. It ain't like him to lie low.'

Halloran grimaced. 'Don't worry about him, Ham. He can take good care of himself.' He stifled a yawn. 'Say, I need a bite to eat and a couple of hours sleep. When it's full light I'll ride into town and have words with Ramsey — see if I can't get at the truth of what happened to the sheriff.'

'I'll ride with you,' Ham said instantly.

Halloran shook his head. 'I expect the Egans will ride in here as soon as the sun shows, and we've got to fight them. So you better get your crew together an hour before dawn and stand ready. It'll be time enough to look for Jeff after we've settled the Egans.'

Ham shrugged. 'I'll rely on your word, Halloran. Why don't you go into the house? Cora is awake. She'll give you food and show you to a bed. I'll call you if the Egans show up. Leave your horse. I'll take care of it in a few minutes.'

Halloran nodded and entered the

house. Asa Deacon was asleep in a big easy chair with a rifle leaning against the wall within reach. Cora was seated at the long table, reading a book. She looked up at Halloran's entrance, and smiled tiredly.

'Did you see Ham outside?' she asked.

'Yeah, and he told me a posse showed up looking for Jeff.'

'They wanted him for killing Sheriff Kett, but I can't believe Jeff would do such a thing.'

'I doubt he did,' Halloran grimaced, 'But we won't get to the bottom of that business until we can talk to Jeff. I'll look for him in the morning. Is that food I can smell on the stove? I'm empty as a bucket with a hole in it.'

'Sit down. I'll get a plate. What happened at the Bar E? Did you shoot any Egans?'

'I tossed a lot of lead at them, but I expect them to ride in here when the sun comes up, thirsting to get their own back, so we'll all have a good chance of shooting at them. How's Tilda?'

'She'll be all right.' There was no sympathy in Cora's tone. She fetched a plate of stew from the stove, set it before Halloran, and he ate hungrily. 'Do you really think the Egans will ride in here openly?'

Halloran nodded. 'They'll come, and we'll be waiting for them; there are enough of us to handle them. We'll cut their numbers down and give them such a beating they won't want to show up here again.'

Cora suppressed a shiver and sat down at the table. She picked up her book but was unable to continue reading and put it aside. Halloran finished his meal and mopped up gravy with a thick slice of bread.

'That was good,' he remarked. 'I need sleep now, but I'd better forget about that. I should take a ride around the ranch to check for trouble. When the shooting starts, pick a window to shoot from, and keep your head down as much as possible; don't try to kill all the Egans yourself.'

'I do know how to fight,' Cora retorted sharply.

Halloran grinned and got up. He went out to the porch and Ham appeared at his side.

'I thought you wanted some sleep?' Ham said.

'It will have to wait.' Halloran looked around. The range was still quiet, but the night sky was losing its density, the stars fading, and the long black shadows were turning grey. 'I'll need a fresh horse, Ham. I want to check the approaches to the spread. We'll need as much warning as we can get when the Egans ride in. Is your crew standing by?'

Ham nodded. 'I don't think anyone has slept during the night — we're ready for anything. There are seven of us, including Pa. I reckon the Egans will need twenty men to crack us, and they ain't got that many on hand so we should hold them. I'll get you a horse. I'm wondering what has happened to

Jeff. That posse must have got him or he would have showed up here by now.'

'I'll wait until after we've discouraged any callers at sunup,' Halloran decided. 'Then I'll ride into town and see if I can pick up his trail.'

He stood on the porch and looked around while Ham fetched him a fresh horse. When he rode out he made a wide circle around the ranch, pausing frequently to look and listen. He heard nothing but the morning breeze in his ears, and satisfied himself that the approaches to Big D were deserted. He returned to the yard, trying to control his tiredness. The horizon to the east was stained pink by the sun just below the skyline. Silence held the range in its grip but Halloran was not fooled by the peacefulness of a new morning. He knew the Egans would be coming pretty soon now, and was impatient for the battle to commence, but he had a nagging doubt in the back of his mind and realized that his concern for Jeff was growing.

Ham was standing in a slight recess at a corner of the house, watching the range in the direction of Bar E, and did not emerge from his position when Halloran reined in at the porch.

'Did you see anyone?' Ham demanded.

'No.' Halloran stifled a yawn. 'Perhaps getting hit in the night has changed their minds about coming here. I reckon I ought to scout in their direction. I should hear them coming a mile off, but we could be wasting our time standing around here. I'm getting worried about Jeff now. He left town last night two jumps ahead of a posse, so where could he be? Knowing him, I reckon he went to the Egan place and probably found trouble there. If that is the case then he's either dead right now or needing a lot of help.'

'I agree,' Ham said worriedly. 'Will you go look for him? I'm certain we can hold this place if the Egans show up.'

'Sure.' Halloran reached a decision

and turned the horse. 'I'll be back soon as I can.'

'Watch your step,' Ham advised.

Halloran nodded and rode across the yard. He loosened his pistol in its holster as he headed through the dawn towards Bar E . . .

Jeff huddled in the grass as slugs thumped around his position. He was finding it difficult to use the rifle one-handed, and despair filled him when the two riders attacking him separated and came at him from different directions. A bullet passed through the crown of his Stetson and jerked it from his head. He held his fire, waiting for the men to draw closer; the man down in the grass was triggering his rifle rapidly, filling the night with noise and flame. A slug struck Jeff a glancing blow along the line of his jaw and his senses fled instantly. He dropped the rifle and lay motionless.

'I think we've got him,' Ramsey called when the shooting died away. 'Keep him covered, Ezra, and I'll get his gun. I ain't taking any chances with him after this.'

Ramsey strode forward with his pistol levelled. He kicked aside Jeff's rifle and bent over his prisoner. Blood was dripping from Jeff's face, and Ramsey grunted as he felt for a heartbeat. Elation filled him when he discovered that Jeff was alive.

'I got him,' he called.

Ezra Egan came forward to level his pistol at Jeff's head. 'I ought to finish him off,' he grated. 'With him outa the way the Deacons are finished.'

'No,' Ramsey said quickly. 'It will be better to have him charged and hanged for Kett's murder. I'll take him back to town now and jail him. Then I can tidy up around the county. If you'll be warned by me you won't ride over to the Big D yet. Give me a chance to work on them legally. With Kett out of the way you might be able to grab the rest of the valley with the help of the law. That would be better than using gun smoke.'

'You'll have to talk to Pa about that,' Ezra replied. 'He's keen to put the Deacons out, and Chris was all set to do the job.'

'But Chris is in town with a bullet in his shoulder,' Ramsey insisted, 'and most of his gang has been wiped out. I reckon my way is easier than going for the Deacons head on. Let's get back to your place and have a powwow with Frank. We'll make him see sense. You've got everything to gain and nothing to lose by doing it my way.'

Ramsey fetched the horses while Ezra checked his brother Ben, who had been hit by Jeff's first shot. Ben was not seriously wounded but there was blood on his upper left arm. 'Have you killed him?' Ben demanded.

'No,' Ezra replied. 'Ramsey wants to jail him, and I think he's right. We've got the law on our side now and Ramsey will do the dirty work for us. Come on, we need to get back to the ranch.'

Ramsey had brought along a spare

horse, and loaded Jeff across its saddle. He was impatient now to get back to town, and was wondering how his posse had made out at Big D.

'Bear in mind what I said,' he told Ezra as they turned back to the ranch. 'No sense starting an all-out shooting war when I can pull a few tricks and get the same result. My way, nobody gets hurt except the Deacons.'

They rode back to Bar E, and found the place in darkness when they entered the yard. A voice called a challenge from the shadows around the house and Ezra growled a reply. Frank Egan stepped on to the porch with a Winchester ready in his hands.

'Where the hell have you been?' Frank demanded. 'Someone sneaked in here a couple of hours ago and shot the hell out of us. Must have tossed thirty slugs into the house and bunk house, and then ran off the horses. Three of the outfit stopped lead — Lanky Childers is dead. The rest of the boys are out rounding up the horse flesh.

When they get back we are heading for Big D. I want all the Deacons dead before breakfast.'

'Get a hold on your temper, Pa,' Ezra said. 'Ramsey has got an idea which will be better than shooting the hell out of the Deacons. Now Kett is dead, Ramsey is in the big saddle as far as the law is concerned, and he can get at the Deacons legally. He's gonna tote Jeff Deacon to jail and charge him with murdering the sheriff.'

'I want the satisfaction of shooting the Deacons myself,' Frank replied. 'We'll keep Jeff Deacon here as a hostage. The Deacons will toe the line if we have him.'

'I want to put him behind bars where he'll be safe,' Ramsey insisted. 'If he's hanged for murdering the sheriff then all the sympathy in the county will be on your side and you'll be able to get away with murder.'

'The gunslinger that turned up in town last night, Halloran,' Frank mused. 'He's hell on wheels. You'll have to take care of him, Ramsey. I reckon it was him here in the night. Cut him out of it and I'll go along with what you say. But do it soon as you can.'

'OK.' Ramsey nodded. 'I'll leave Deacon here in your hands and ride over to Big D to put Halloran down in the dust. It'll be a simple matter to say he was involved in helping a killer escape. Then I'll come back for Deacon, jail him, and charge him with Kett's murder.'

'You ain't even sure the sheriff is dead yet,' Frank observed. 'How the hell can you charge him with murder if Kett is still breathing?'

'That's just a detail.' Ramsey grinned. 'I told you to leave everything to me.'

Frank Egan grimaced. 'Well, you've got your chance,' he said. 'We'll hold our fire until you get back here. If you don't get Halloran then we'll ride into Big D and wipe them Deacons out.'

'See you later.' Ramsey handed the reins of Jeff's horse to Ezra and swung his mount to ride out. He headed north towards Big D. Dawn was crowding the range now; the sky to the east was tinged with the first probing rays of the rising sun, and heat was beginning to make its presence felt.

As he rode, Ramsey considered the situation. He had attacked Sheriff Kett on an impulse, and it was looking like he could settle the blame on Jeff Deacon. He wanted to get in good with the Egans, and planned to use them for personal gain when their trouble with the Deacons was settled. He sensed that he had good reason to feel satisfied with events. With Jeff out of the way the Deacons would fall by the wayside, and there could be rich pickings around the county with the Egans on his side. He was aware that they had been rustling stock from some of their neighbours, and he wanted his cut for services rendered.

The sun showed above the horizon and full daylight hit the range. Ramsey followed a slight trail that would take him into the Deacon front yard, and he was about five miles from the spread when his horse stumbled just below a crest and then began to limp. Cursing, Ramsey dismounted to examine the animal's left fetlock. He was bent over, lifting the offending hoof, when a rider came over the crest and had to rein aside quickly to avoid a collision. Ramsey sprang up in shock, his right hand dropping to the butt of his holstered pistol.

'You don't need a gun,' Halloran called. He sat his mount, holding the reins in his left hand; his right hand flat on his upper right thigh, within distance of the black butt showing in his holster.

'Who in hell are you?' Ramsey blustered. 'Do you ride for Big D?'

Halloran saw the deputy sheriff star on Ramsey's shirt front and wondered where Jeff was. It didn't look like the crooked deputy had arrested him yet.

'No,' Halloran bluffed. 'I'm not a Big D rider, although I had breakfast there earlier. I'm on my way to Plainsville.'

'What's your business? You don't

look like a cowpoke to me. If you're a gunslinger looking for a job then I advise you to try another county. The Deacons are gonna lose the fight they've got coming up, and the Egans don't need gun help.'

'I heard at Big D that a posse is out looking for Jeff Deacon. They said Deacon killed the sheriff in Plainsville. Is that a fact?'

'You got the right of it.' Ramsey lifted his hand from the butt of his pistol. 'Is the posse still at Big D?'

Halloran shook his head. 'They left hours before I got there.'

'And they didn't show up at Bar E,' Ramsey mused. 'So they must have ridden back to town.'

'You've been at the Egan place?' Halloran tensed the fingers of his right hand. 'Is Jeff Deacon there?'

'What would he be doing there? The Egans are out to kill all Deacons.' Ramsey narrowed his eyes as he peered closely at Halloran. 'What's your interest in Jeff Deacon if you're just riding through?'

'I heard talk at the Deacon ranch. They think the Egans must have grabbed him.'

'Well, I didn't see him there.' Ramsey shook his head. 'Jeff Deacon has got a sidekick named Halloran. Did you see him at Big D?'

'I saw a dozen tough cowpokes that are ready for a fight but I didn't get any names.'

'So what's your name?'

Halloran saw suspicion flaring in Ramsey's eyes. He grinned. 'I'm Clint Halloran,' he admitted. 'It's easy to see whose side you're on in this trouble. Who really killed Sheriff Kett? And don't tell me it was Jeff because I won't believe you.'

'I saw Jeff Deacon kill the sheriff,' Ramsey said through his teeth. 'Are you calling me a liar?'

'Yeah, that's right.' Halloran nodded. 'You're a liar right through to your backbone, mister. So if you're blaming Jeff for killing the sheriff, and you were there when Kett was killed, then you must be the killer, because, like I said, Jeff wouldn't raise a hand against a law man.'

Ramsey reached for his gun in a fast draw. The pistol came out of his holster smoothly, and he was cocking it when he realized that Halloran had beaten him to the draw. He became aware that he was staring into the muzzle of Halloran's gun and halted his play.

'You've got a choice,' Halloran said. 'Drop it or try to use it. Either way your job as a deputy ends right here. What's it gonna be?'

Ramsey opened his fingers and his gun fell into the dust. He sat gazing at Halloran like a prairie dog looking at a preying rattlesnake; his eyes filled with shock.

'So where is Jeff?' Halloran demanded.

'I told you I ain't seen him. You're making a big mistake, Halloran, pointing a gun at me.'

'Why are you riding into Big D?'

'I need to talk to Asa Deacon,'

Ramsey bluffed. 'The sheriff was keen on avoiding bloodshed in the valley, and I'm aiming for the same thing. So you better put up your gun and clear out before I decide to stick you behind bars.'

Halloran was aware that taking Ramsey prisoner would limit his activities and prove to be embarrassing. He could tell by the deputy's expression and demeanour that he was a bad enemy of the Deacons. He motioned with his gun.

'You'd better get the hell out of here,' he said. 'You're the one should make tracks out of the county. I heard that you are wanted for robbery with violence in Abilene. So make yourself scarce and stay out of this trouble. If I see you around after this I'll shoot you on sight.'

Ramsey shrugged. 'I'm leaving,' he said. 'But I'll see you again, Halloran, and next time I'll be holding the gun.'

'Get rid of your rifle before you leave.' Halloran waited until Ramsey had pulled his Winchester out of its boot and dropped it. 'Now split the breeze, and remember my warning. Don't let me see you again.'

Ramsey turned his horse and rode off in the direction of the Egan place. Halloran sat watching him until he was out of sight. He guessed Jeff was being held prisoner at the Egan ranch, and set out to trail the deputy, staying well back. Ramsey's horse seemed to be lame and made slow progress. The sun was high in the heavens when Ramsey finally rode into the Egan yard. Halloran dismounted behind a skyline to conceal himself and his horse and watched patiently for developments, expecting Ramsey to head for town with Jeff as his prisoner.

But it was several hours later when the seemingly deserted ranch showed signs of activity. Four men suddenly emerged from the house and paused on the porch. Halloran, now chafing with impatience at his long wait, saw that one of them was Jeff. His sidekick was

183

unsteady on his feet; left arm strapped to his side and blood staining his shirt and leather vest. Ramsey was there, and he led his limping horse across to the corral accompanied by Frank Egan, whom Halloran had last seen in the sheriff's office the night before, drinking whiskey with Kett. The fourth man was holding a pistol in his right hand, covering Jeff, who sat down heavily in a rocking chair on the porch.

Halloran waited interminably. Ramsey transferred his saddle to a fresh horse and then saddled another mount. He was talking seriously to Frank Egan, who kept shaking his head in apparent disagreement until they returned to the house. Jeff was made to mount one of the horses and Ramsey swung into his saddle. Halloran sighed with relief when Ramsey set out across the yard, leading Jeff's horse. When the deputy had disappeared beyond the house, Halloran, frustrated by his enforced inactivity over several nail-biting hours, fetched his mount and rode in a wide circle around the ranch, intent on rescuing Jeff from the crooked deputy.

Ramsey reached the outskirts of Plainsville as the heat of the day faded and night drew on. Halloran remained in the background. He was concerned about confronting Ramsey because it was a situation which would be difficult to resolve. He would have to shoot Ramsey or disarm him and hold him prisoner, and neither course appealed. Halloran watched Ramsey ride along the street towards the law office. The sun was well over in the west and there were few folk on the street. Halloran dismounted at a hitch-rail and continued on foot. When Ramsey passed the saloon a man emerged through the batwings and stood on the sidewalk gazing after the deputy and his prisoner.

Halloran saw another man emerge from an alley opposite the law office and recognized Mack Egan. The man in front of the saloon stepped down into the street and walked quickly towards the law office. Halloran recognized a gun trap instantly and dropped his hand to his pistol. Before he could intervene, Mack Egan stepped into the dust of the street. Ramsey was in the act of dragging Jeff out of his saddle.

'Hold it, Ramsey,' Mack Egan called. 'What are you gonna do with Deacon?'

Ramsey's head jerked round and he gazed impassively at Mack.

'Why do you wanta know?' Ramsey demanded. 'I'm doing my job so get the hell outa here. I've arrested Deacon for killing the sheriff. Why ain't you out at Bar E with your folks?'

The man who had emerged from the saloon paused and dropped his right hand to the butt of his holstered pistol. 'Turn Deacon loose and put a gun in his hand, Ramsey,' he called. 'That buzzard put a slug in me last night and I wanta let daylight through him.'

'Cut it out, Chris,' Ramsey replied. 'I need Deacon behind bars. He's facing a charge of murder and I wanta see him hang for it.'

Halloran caught a glimpse of movement on the far side of the deputy, and recognized Doc Woollard emerging from his office.

'Ramsey,' the doc called. 'Who did Jeff kill?'

The deputy half turned to bring the doctor into his line of vision. 'Stay back, Doc,' he replied. 'I'm busy right now. I'll see you later.'

'Talk to me now, Ramsey,' Woollard insisted.

'I told you last night that Deacon knifed the sheriff,' Ramsey said.

'That's so,' Woollard agreed, 'and Kett died in the early hours of this morning. But he regained consciousness just before midnight, and made a statement before witnesses, naming you as his assailant, Ramsey. You stabbed the sheriff and caused his death, not Jeff Deacon.'

Ramsey froze momentarily. He glanced around the street and saw several townsmen appearing from cover with levelled weapons all pointing at him. He looked over his shoulder for a way of escape like a cornered coyote and saw Halloran at his back. His expression changed to one of desperation as he made a play for his gun . . .

8

Halloran stepped off the sidewalk and angled to put Chris Egan out of his line of fire. When he saw Ramsey's gun clear leather he flowed into action, but out of the corner of his eye he saw Mack Egan reach for his holstered pistol, and yelled for the youngster to stay out of it. Ramsey cleared leather and swung his weapon to cover Jeff. Halloran fired, aiming for Ramsey's pistol, and his slug struck the weapon, sending it flying through the air. Ramsey grasped Jeff, who was standing helplessly beside his horse, and held him as a shield against further shooting. Blood showed on the fingers of his right hand, but he reached into his left-hand pocket, produced a small .38 two-shot weapon and pressed the muzzle against Jeff's neck.

'Deacon will get it if you don't haul off,' Ramsey yelled. 'Everybody stand still. Get rid of your guns. I'll ride out of here and you won't see me again.'

'No dice, Ramsey,' Doc Woollard replied. 'The town has had enough of this trouble and we are going to ensure that it ends here and now. Throw down that gun or you'll be shot dead.'

'I ain't bluffing,' Ramsey snarled. 'I know when the game is up so I'll skedaddle. If you want Deacon alive then get the hell away from here.'

Halloran was covering Ramsey but could not get a clear shot at the deputy's pistol and held his fire. Jeff was hung over; helpless with a gun muzzle pressing against the side of his neck. He sagged in Ramsey's desperate grip and the deputy was forced to exert his strength to hold him upright. Chris Egan remained motionless, mindful of Halloran at his back, and Mack Egan stood holding his pistol, wanting to get into the action but unable to decide.

'Clint, I know you're here,' Jeff called to Halloran. 'I heard your voice. Let Ramsey ride out of town with me. I'll take my chance with him, and you can trail him later and get him. He's a killer, so don't take any chances. Give him his head and he'll clear out of the county.'

'It is out of your hands, Jeff,' Halloran replied. 'Ramsey is finished around here, and the only place he is going is behind bars. What about it, Ramsey? You've got a choice, such as it is. Give up or shoot Jeff and die with him. I ain't fooling. I got the drop on you and this will go my way.'

Ramsey considered the situation. He sensed that Halloran was not bluffing, and could see only one way out. If he went to jail the Egans might show up and bust him loose. He threw his pistol to the ground and raised his hands. Halloran passed Chris Egan, pulling the man's gun from its holster in passing.

'You'll stand still if you know what's good for you,' Halloran told Chris. 'Get your hands up.'

Townsmen came forward with levelled guns and Ramsey was seized and bundled into the law office. Halloran motioned for Chris Egan to follow Ramsey, and turned to Mack Egan, who had holstered his gun.

'Are you serious about Tilda Deacon, Mack?' Halloran asked.

'Sure I am,' Mack replied.

'She was shot by one of the Egan outfit last night on her way back to Big D. You're on the wrong side of the fence if you care for that girl.'

'Is she bad hurt?' Mack demanded.

'She'll live, I reckon.'

'I'll ride out to the Deacon place and see her,' Mack decided. 'I've never been in this fight against the Deacons, and I won't take sides now.'

'It wouldn't be wise to visit the valley right now; not with the Deacon outfit ready to shoot the minute they see an Egan.'

'There won't be any more trouble if Chris is kept behind bars,' Mack responded. 'He's the one been pushing for action. He came in here on the dodge with his gang of bank robbers, and they've kept the pot boiling just for

192

the pure hell of it. Keep Chris out of it and the trouble will fade away.'

'I don't think you're right,' Halloran mused. 'It's a cat and dog business. The Deacons and the Egans are natural enemies, and men have been killed on both sides. I don't think either family would back down now.'

'I'll ride out to Bar E and talk to my pa. He'll see sense when I tell him what's happened here.'

Halloran studied the youngster's face and saw good intention in his expression. 'You can try it, but I think you'll have the ride for nothing. Now get out of here, and stay out of trouble, if you can.'

Mack nodded and turned away. Halloran watched him for a moment, and then entered the law office. Ramsey and Chris Egan had been taken into the cells. Jeff was seated on a chair at the desk, his head resting in his hands, and Doc Woollard was bending over him. Two hard-faced townsmen stood in the background, both holding pistols. The doc looked up at Halloran.

'I'll take Jeff over to my office,' he said. 'I reckon he'll need a couple of weeks to get over this wound. Jack Brewster, there, is the town blacksmith, and he's gonna take over as a temporary sheriff until we can get a dependable man in to do the job. There'll be no more trouble in town after this.'

Halloran looked at Brewster, a big man with wide shoulders and brawny arms whose face showed determination.

'I wish you luck,' Halloran said. 'It's the Egans you'll have to watch out for. None of the Deacons will come looking for trouble.'

'There won't be any trouble from either side,' Brewster said in a voice that sounded like gravel rolling in the bottom of a creek. 'Now we've stepped in we won't go for half-measures. We know who is pushing for violence, and we'll come down hard on anyone that doesn't toe the line after this.'

'That's good to hear,' Halloran

observed. 'You can call on me if you need a fast gun to back your play.'

'Thanks for the offer.' Brewster nodded. 'But I reckon the town has got to handle this. I heard you say that Ramsey is wanted for robbery with violence in Abilene.'

'That's what I heard. It should be easy to check out.'

'We'll contact the law in Abilene and tell them we've got Ramsey in jail,' said Doc Woollard. 'But we've got a charge of murder for him to face. It's lucky for Jeff that Sheriff Kett regained consciousness last night.'

'His statement set us all moving.' Brewster nodded. 'And Chris Egan has robbed his last bank.'

Halloran grimaced. He did not think the situation would ease, but was prepared to go along with the change of mood gripping the town. He had seen it happen before in towns through the West, but sometimes townsfolk became too zealous in promoting law and order.

'Give me a hand with Jeff,' Woollard

said, motioning to Halloran. 'Is there any danger of Big D being attacked by the Egans?'

'I was expecting the Egans to take to the warpath last night,' Halloran replied as he slid an arm under Jeff's left elbow and helped him to his feet. 'I took some action which might have put them off for a spell, but I wouldn't count on it. We'll head back to Big D soon as you've finished with Jeff.'

'He won't be fit to ride for a couple of weeks,' Woollard said firmly. 'You'll have to leave him here in town until he's stronger.'

'No dice, Doc,' Jeff said determinedly. 'I need to be at the ranch just in case the Egans do show up.'

Halloran looked keenly at Jeff and realized that the doctor was right. Jeff wouldn't be riding anywhere for at least a week. They eased Jeff through the office door to the sidewalk, and Halloran dropped a hand to his pistol when he heard the sound of hoofs approaching rapidly along the street.

His teeth clicked together when he recognized Cora Deacon riding in; the girl's haste warned him that she was the bearer of bad news.

'It's Cora,' Jeff observed, straightening and shifting his weight from Halloran's arm. 'Something's wrong at the ranch. Give me a gun, Clint, and let's get moving.'

'Hold on until we've heard what Cora has to say,' Halloran responded.

Cora spotted them and turned her horse in to the sidewalk. Her face was pale, and she was badly shocked.

'I was hoping to find you here, Doc,' she said, leaning her hands on her saddle horn. She closed her eyes and took several deep breaths. 'Some of the Egans turned up at Big D at noon and there was shooting. Ham is hurt bad, and Pa took a bullet in his left side. I don't think Pa will live. I had to take the long trail in because of the Egans. Can you ride back to the ranch with me?'

Halloran was already moving to

where he had tethered his horse. As he swung into the saddle Jeff went by him, spurring a horse mercilessly. Cora followed her brother, raising dust in the street. As Halloran went after them, Doc Woollard shouted after him.

'I'll follow you,' he yelled, 'and I'll bring a posse along.'

Halloran lifted a hand in acknowledgement and hammered out of town to catch up with Jeff and Cora. Jeff was swaying in his saddle and Halloran doubted that he would be able to maintain the fast pace all the way to the ranch. They followed the trail north. Halloran was better mounted and began to forge ahead. He glanced at Jeff as he swept by brother and sister. Jeff was white-faced and looked about ready to fall from his saddle, but his grim determination was readily apparent.

'I'll go on ahead,' Halloran called. 'Take it easy, Jeff, and don't leave Cora alone.'

Jeff nodded. His teeth were clamped

together, his jaw set in dogged determination, but his flesh had been weakened by his wound and his efforts were flagging. His eyes filled with despair as he faced up to his weakness, but he stayed in his saddle and rode with all the experience he could muster.

Halloran pulled away and urged his horse to more effort. He watched his surroundings as he galloped north, expecting an ambush along the trail to the valley. When he reached the Egan range he drew his pistol and held it in his hand. A sudden movement ahead and to his left had him lifting his gun, for, as he expected, the Egans were waiting. Two riders appeared on a crest and began to approach him at an angle to intercept him.

Instead of trying to avoid the men, Halloran went for them, aware that Jeff and Cora were coming along behind and Jeff was in no position to defend himself or his sister. He could see that one of the riders was an Egan but did not remember the man's name, only that he was big and black-bearded. It was probably Burt Egan, Frank's brother, and Halloran cocked his pistol and prepared to fight.

Egan started shooting, and his slugs crackled around Halloran with surprising accuracy. Halloran squeezed his trigger and gun smoke blew back in his face. He aimed at Egan, and saw the man jerk in his saddle before falling forward over his saddle horn. Halloran turned his gun on the second man, but the rider ducked, reached out to grab Egan's reins, and set off back over the crest. Halloran let them go, and did not slow his horse as he continued towards the still distant Big D.

Two hours later Halloran topped a rise and saw the Deacon ranch. He glanced along his back trail but there was no sign of Jeff and Cora. Gun in hand, he urged his tiring mount forward and rode into the yard. The ranch was seemingly deserted, with an air of brooding hostility in its stillness. He looked around keenly, and saw no horses in the corral. That troubled him, but then he spotted movement in the doorway of the house and lifted his gun to cover the figure that appeared on the porch. It was Asa Deacon, and the old man's shirt was soaked in blood. The rancher was holding a rifle, and he leaned against the door jamb when he recognized Halloran.

'Buck and Ezra Egan were here with a couple of their outfit,' Asa said as he dropped heavily into the rocking chair on the porch. He placed the rifle across his knees. 'They tried to blast the place apart, but we chased them off eventually. Ham is down with a bullet in his shoulder, and I took one in the side.'

'Cora rode into town,' Halloran said. 'She thought you were like to die.'

'I guess I must have looked pretty bad at that,' Asa said humourlessly. 'I bled a lot and that scared the girl. Have you seen Jeff?'

'He's on his way back here with Cora. Ramsey had captured him but I got him loose. Was anybody else hurt in the shooting?'

'No. Mitchell and the outfit took out after Buck and Ezra. I ain't seen them since.'

'I think it was Burt Egan I winged back along the trail. I saw him in town when I arrived. He was under arrest then, with his brother Frank, but they were turned loose. How is Tilda?'

'She'll live.' Asa's chin touched his chest and he found it difficult to remain in a sitting position on the chair.

Halloran dismounted. 'I'll take care of my horse and then stand by here until the doc and a posse show. Ramsey is in jail for murdering Sheriff Kett.'

'The posse was in here last night accusing Jeff of killing the sheriff,' Asa said in an outraged tone. 'Can't they make up their minds about who did it?'

'Kett recovered consciousness before he died and made a statement accusing Ramsey of stabbing him.'

'Ramsey is a low-down hound! And he had the nerve to ride in here and

202

blame my boy!' Asa sagged in the rocker and closed his eyes.

Halloran dropped his reins and stepped on to the porch. He bent over Asa. Blood was seeping from the wound in the old man's side.

'Let me take a look at you,' Halloran said. 'The doc will be here soon with a posse, but we'd better stop you bleeding.'

'I'll be all right.' Asa made an effort to sit upright. His craggy face was pale; his eyes over-bright. 'But I could do with a drink of water. Would you get some from the kitchen?'

'Sure.' Halloran holstered his pistol and pushed open the door of the house. He stepped inside and paused on the threshold, his gaze flickering around the big room. Mrs Deacon was sitting at the big table with Tilda at her side, both grim-faced and silent. Ham Deacon was lying on a couch across the room, asleep or unconscious.

Halloran frowned. 'What are you doing up, Tilda?' he demanded.

The door swung to with considerable force, striking Halloran's left shoulder. His quick reflexes took him a pace to his right and he turned to face the door as it slammed, reaching for his pistol as he did so. A big black-bearded figure lunged forward from behind the door, swinging a pistol, and Halloran tried to avoid the attack. Egan's gun barrel slammed against Halloran's skull before he could draw his pistol.

Egan struck again and Halloran fell, his senses whirling. He reached out to grab at Egan, but was hit yet again, and Halloran pitched forward on to his face and relaxed inertly.

9

Night had fallen when Mack Egan rode out of Plainsville. He reined in on the outskirts of the town and looked back along the street, his thoughts teeming with the knowledge that Chris Egan was behind bars, and that most of gang of bank robbers his cousin operated had been killed. Mack heaved a sigh of relief at the turn of events. Perhaps now there was a chance that the trouble in Sunset Valley would die naturally without Chris prodding and niggling at it all the time. His thoughts turned to Tilda Deacon, and he spurred his horse and rode on to Bar E. He needed to talk with his father; Frank might just listen to sense now Chris was behind bars.

He had done much thinking since Tilda had ridden back to the Deacon ranch with Halloran the night before.

He was in love with Tilda, but the pressures of being an Egan had far outweighed his personal feelings and he had not dared admit his emotions to himself or his family. But the difference that Halloran's arrival made to the Deacons had opened his eyes to the realities of the situation and he knew he could not remain inactive while the family of the girl he loved was wiped out. He had to make a stand whatever the outcome. The trouble had to stop immediately, and he was of a mind to turn his gun on his own family if they did not see reason and call a halt to their actions.

When he heard the sound of a rider travelling fast to town he turned aside and sat his mount in cover, wondering what else had happened on the range. No one rode so fast at night unless there was an emergency, and he watched the rider hammering by on the trail. He bent low to silhouette the figure against the starry sky, and frowned when he recognized Cora

Deacon. What was her hurry? He stifled an impulse to intercept the girl and continued towards the Egan ranch.

Lights were burning in the ranch house when he reached Bar E and he entered the yard openly, aware that a guard would be posted. The Egans were taking no chances with the Deacons after pushing for trouble. His father called to him as he approached the porch, and he replied before continuing. Frank Egan came forward out of the shadows with a rifle cradled in his arms.

'What are you doing here?' Frank demanded. 'I heard you got shot bad in town.'

'It ain't too bad,' Mack replied. 'All hell broke loose when Ramsey rode in herding Jeff Deacon in handcuffs.' He went on to explain the situation in town. 'It looks like Doc Woollard has got the townsfolk fired up about the trouble. Ramsey has been jailed, and so has Uncle Chris. Halloran said Ramsey is wanted for robbery with violence in

Abilene, and Woollard said Sheriff Kent regained consciousness before he died and made a statement saying Ramsey stabbed him, not Jeff Deacon.'

'The hell you say! And they stuck Chris behind bars? Why didn't you stop them? With Chris out of circulation we are out on a limb.'

'There was nothing I could do.' Mack shrugged. 'Halloran showed up behind Ramsey and shot a gun out of Ramsey's hand. Halloran is hell on wheels! I reckon you better forget about the trouble. There's no way we can go against the whole county if it gets up on its hind legs to stop us. Ramsey was our ace in the hole but it looks like he's out of it now, and Chris and his bunch came off second best when Halloran started operating for the Deacons.'

'By sunup the trouble will be over,' Frank said heavily. 'Buck and Ezra rode out to Big D after someone showed up here earlier and shot us up. I guess the Deacons will be finished by now, and good riddance to them.'

'You let them go up the valley to kill the Deacons?' Mack demanded. 'What's got into you, Pa? Hell, you've gone too far! You'll never get away with it. I've come to try and talk you out of making more trouble.'

'You're too late. It's time we finished it. But you've never liked the idea of fighting it out, Mack, and I reckoned it was because of that Deacon gal.'

'What did you tell Buck and Ezra to do?' Mack demanded.

'They know what to do without being told. Like I said, come sunup the trouble will be over.'

'You're a fool, Pa! I'd better ride up to Big D and stop Buck and Ezra.' Mack reined about to ride back across the yard, and heard the metallic click of Frank's rifle being cocked.

'Stay where you are, Mack,' Frank snapped. 'Get off that horse and come into the house. You ain't going anywhere.'

Mack paused and looked down at his father. Frank's face was in shadow, but there was no mistaking the menace in his attitude, and the muzzle of his Winchester pointed at Mack's chest. Mack laughed mirthlessly.

'Are you gonna shoot me if I don't?' he demanded.

'You and that damned Deacon gal!' Frank growled. 'She's got you hogtied and blinded, you fool! You've been hankering after her for a long time, and there ain't no way she'll look at you after the trouble we've given her family. So stop acting loco and get off that horse before I shoot you out of the saddle.'

Mack stared down at his father, his temper flaring. 'If that's the way you feel then you better pull the trigger,' he grated. 'I never wanted anything to do with trouble but you've got a bee in your bonnet about the Deacons and you'll keep on pushing them until it's shoot on sight between our families. Well, I ain't had any part of it, and I'm riding out now. You'll have to shoot me if you wanta stop me, Pa, because I ain't sticking around here any longer, and I won't come back until you sort out this trouble.'

He turned away from the porch and touched spurs to the flanks of his horse.

'I'm warning you,' Frank called. 'You better do like I say. Come back here, Mack.'

Mack clenched his teeth and kept riding. Frank stared after him, fighting the wild impulse that surged through him. He lifted the rifle and put pressure on the trigger.

'Pull up, Mack,' he advised.

Mack did not reply or look round. He pushed his horse into a canter and continued across the yard. Frank cursed and fired a shot skywards. Mack was startled and spurred his horse. He rode out of the yard, expecting another shot, but gun echoes faded across the range and he vanished into the shadows without further incident. Frank listened to the receding hoof beats, filled with rage by his son's disobedience. He lowered the Winchester and went back into the house.

Mack rode fast through the night, his thoughts on Tilda Deacon. At last he had made a stand about his feelings for the girl, and knew there could be no going back. He only hoped he would not be too late arriving at the Deacon spread to prevent his brothers carrying out Frank's orders.

A mile to Mack's right and two miles ahead of him, Jeff and Cora Deacon were riding in the same direction. Jeff was finding it harder to stay in his saddle with every fresh step his horse took. His wound was debilitating; he clung to his saddle horn, his eyes closed. He was barely aware of his surroundings. Cora's reassuring voice kept cutting into his dulled thoughts, urging him to hang on over the last miles to the ranch, and he tried to obey her desperate commands, but inch by inch he slipped from his jolting saddle until he reached the point of no return and pitched sideways to the ground. He was unconscious when Cora joined him, and she gazed despairingly at his limp figure as she tried to bring him back to his senses.

Five miles back along the trail, Doc Woollard and his five-man posse galloped through the night towards Big D. Having taken the initiative in Plainsville, Woollard was determined to uphold the law. Sheriff Kett had not been a strong lawman; had shown sympathy towards the Egans on several occasions, and Woollard was prepared to go as far as necessary to redress Kett's shortcomings, the worst of which had been the sheriff's blatant acceptance of Dan Ramsey despite Ramsey's obvious disregard for the law.

Ramsey sat in his cell in town and regarded Chris Egan in the next cell with an inscrutable gaze. Ramsey had never liked Chris, mainly because Chris was well established in his particular line of outlawry and could not be controlled. But Chris was lounging on his bunk as if he hadn't a care in the world; he had even exchanged jokes with Brewster, the temporary sheriff, when he had been locked in the cell, and in the hour since their incarceration, Ramsey had overheard Chris occasionally humming a tune. Ramsey was ready to snatch any opportunity to escape, but guessed there would be no chances at all with the new law man acting like a cat on hot bricks.

'What are you so cheerful about, Chris?' Ramsey demanded at length. 'You're facing twenty years in prison for what you've done.'

'It'll never happen,' Chris replied with a grin. 'I've got a couple of men in town who will bust me out of here as soon as they get the word about me. If you've got any dough stashed away then it'll cost you one hundred bucks to walk out with me, and bear in mind that you're gonna hang if you stick around here.'

'I don't have anyone out there willing to help me,' Ramsey replied, 'and I don't need anyone. I haven't seen a jail yet that could hold me when I'm ready to leave. I've spent hours here in the front office, mostly nights, whiling away the time by making a couple of keys which are stitched in the lining of my jacket — one to fit the cell locks and one that will open the back door. I reckon on leaving any time now.'

'Is that a fact?' Egan grimaced. 'Now that is what I call being prepared. What will it cost me to leave with you?'

'What would you do if you got out of here before sunup? Are you gonna waste your time trying to wipe out the Deacons?'

'No.' Chris shook his head. 'I'm gonna get me another gang and go back to robbing banks, which is a whole lot easier than bossing a range war. What are your plans?'

'I'm finished around here.' Ramsey shrugged. 'If Kett made a statement pinning his stabbing on me then I'll have to make tracks for other parts. I'll throw in my lot with you to pick up some easy dough. What do you say?'

'That's OK by me. It's a deal. Let's get out of here now, huh?'

'Sure.' Ramsey grinned. 'I'm ready. It looks like it is gonna be a long, hard day tomorrow.'

Ramsey took the two keys out of the lining of his coat and peered through the bars into Chris Egan's cell. He was unlocking the door of his cell by the time Egan sat up and reached for his Stetson. Ramsey grinned as his cell door opened noiselessly, and he unlocked Egan's cell.

The jail was silent, dimly lit by a guttering lantern. Ramsey went to the back door and unlocked it. A sigh gusted through him when he stuck his head outside and smelled the night breeze. He turned to speak to Chris Egan and saw light coming through the doorway connecting the cells with the front office.

'Someone is opening the door to the office,' Ramsey hissed.

Chris turned instantly as the door in question began to open. Lamplight from the front office shafted into the cells. Chris moved fast despite his wound and, as the massive figure of Brewster came through the doorway, he threw a left-hand punch at the temporary sheriff's solid jaw. Brewster staggered but did not go down, and Chris struck again, throwing his weight behind the blow. Brewster took the second punch and his knees buckled, but he reached out with his powerful hands and grasped Chris by the neck. Chris dropped to his knees, punching desperately with his left fist at the bigger man's jaw. But he was helpless in Brewster's grasp.

Ramsey ran forward and rabbit-punched Brewster, and then kicked him behind the left knee. The blacksmith dropped to the floor as his leg went from under him. Ramsey struck him again and, when Brewster went down on his back, kicked him in the head. He repeated the action until Brewster relaxed into unconsciousness.

'What brought him in here?' Ramsey

demanded as he grasped Chris by the collar and hauled him to his feet. 'Come on. Let's put him in a cell and then we'll get out of here.'

They manhandled Brewster into a cell and Ramsey locked the door. Chris went into the front office and made for the gun rack on the wall behind the desk.

'We need guns,' Chris observed. 'And here's my belt and pistol.' He took the cartridge belt and swung it around his waist, cursing when the movement hurt his wound. He drew the pistol and checked it, his harsh laugh echoing in the office.

Ramsey picked up a gun rig and buckled it around his waist.

'Now we need a couple of horses,' he said. 'We'd better go out the back door and along the back lots.'

They left the jail and angled through the shadows to the rear of the livery barn. The town was quiet. The moon was riding high in the sky to the west. Ramsey was satisfied that they were in time to beat any early risers among the town's population. They located their horses in the barn, saddled up, and left town noiselessly. When they reached the open range, Egan reined in.

'Doggone it! I can't run out on my family,' he said. 'They need my help to beat the Deacons. I'll have to see it through before I can shake the dust of this range off my boots.'

'No sweat,' Ramsey replied. 'I'll ride with you. I've got a couple of debts to repay — Jeff Deacon and Halloran. With them gone the Deacons won't put up much of a fight.'

'The doc said he was gonna ride out to Big D with a posse,' Chris observed. 'If he's still sticking his nose in then we'll have a big fight on our hands.'

'If we take them by surprise they won't know what hit them,' Ramsey said harshly.

'You might even get rid of the murder charge they've got against you.' Chris grinned.

'So let's make tracks.' Ramsey spurred

his horse and started along the trail. 'We need to make good time,' he observed. 'It'll be sunup before we get to Big D.'

When Halloran began to take notice of his surroundings again he realized that he was lying on the floor in the Big D ranch house. Tilda Deacon was bending over him, shaking his shoulder with her left hand. He looked up at her ashen face, saw shock and pain in her eyes, and wondered what had hit him.

'I'm sorry, Halloran,' Tilda said. 'Egan made Pa come out to you with an empty rifle to bluff you into thinking everything was OK in here. He said he'd shoot all of us if Pa didn't do like he said.'

'OK, get away from him,' a harsh voice cut in. 'He's coming round.'

The sound of the voice opened up a fresh trail of thought in Halloran's mind. He turned his head slightly and brought the black-bearded face of one of the Egans into his line of sight — Buck or Ezra, he didn't know which. Halloran frowned as darting pangs of agony stabbed through his head. He realized that he was having difficulty seeing with his left eye, and felt the stickiness of blood on his forehead and cheek. Egan was waving the gun with which he had struck Halloran.

'You made a big mistake coming back,' Egan said. 'Big man with a gun, they said. When you show up you'll wipe us Egans off the face of the earth, they said.' He laughed and cocked his pistol. 'I've a mind to blow your head off right now, mister.'

Tilda cried out in protest. Halloran raised his left hand to his head and explored the area where it had been struck. Blood had leaked from a scalp wound. He closed his eyes, needing time to recover from the blow, and his mind was attuned to getting the better of his captor.

'I guess I can wait until the rest of my family show up,' Egan said. 'There's no need to hurry. The Bar E outfit will get here any time now.'

Halloran glanced around with his

right eye, and saw Asa Deacon sitting on a chair across the room, still holding the Winchester. Despair hit Halloran when he realized the gun was not loaded. The old man looked beaten. His shirt was stained with blood and he seemed to be on his last legs. But Halloran's mind began working smoothly again. He slumped on the floor as if he was exhausted, but he watched Egan intently, hoping for an opportunity to reverse the situation.

'Get up, Halloran,' Egan ordered. 'You're only a hired gun. I can put you away now and no one will miss you. Do you know your pard Jeff Deacon went to town under arrest? Dan Ramsey took him in for killing Sheriff Kett. There'll be one helluva neck-tie party when they hang Jeff.'

Halloran said nothing about the incidents that had occurred in town. The less the Egans knew of the true situation the better. He wondered how far behind him Jeff and Cora were, and hoped Jeff would not ride into the ranch without first checking for trouble.

'I told you to get up!' Buck Egan came to Halloran's side and grasped him with his left hand, sticking the muzzle of his pistol against Halloran's chest as he pulled him upright. 'I'm of a mind to give it to you right now. It was you shot up our spread during the night. I'm gonna make you mighty sorry you ever came into this neck of the woods.'

Halloran began to bunch his muscles to resist despite the gun prodding him, but the front door banged and he glanced around to see yet another Egan, armed with a rifle, entering the big room.

'Buck, I can hear riders coming,' Ezra said. 'We better see who's on the move.'

'It'll be our outfit,' Buck replied confidently. 'I'm gonna take this gun-slinger out back and put a hole in his brisket. How many riders are coming?'

'No more than two. Are you gonna kill all the Deacons?'

'Does that worry you?'

'Hell, no! But Mack is kind of sweet on that gal Tilda. You better not do anything to her in case Mack won't like it.'

'There are plenty more girls around he can pick from.' Buck grinned. 'Go check those riders coming in.'

Ezra grimaced and went out, slamming the door. Buck shook Halloran and jabbed him with the gun muzzle. Halloran straightened, his left hand shooting out, thrusting aside the gun, and his right fist swung in a short arc. His knuckles thudded against Buck's chin as he wrenched the pistol out of the man's hand. Buck tried to resist but the blow to his chin rattled his senses and he tried to throw his arms around Halloran. But the pistol swung and slammed against his head and he fell like an axed tree, out cold.

Halloran staggered as he went to the door and jerked it open. Ezra was standing on the porch, and turned at the sound of the door creaking.

'Say, Buck, I don't hear those riders now,' he said. He paused, and then tried to swing his rifle around to cover Halloran. 'Hey, you ain't Buck!' he yelled.

Halloran fired. The bullet smacked into Ezra's chest. Ezra screeched and went sprawling, losing his grip on the rifle. The echoes of the shot hammered away across the range. Halloran looked around. He could see nothing in the greying dawn and wondered who was out there.

'Jeff,' he called.

'Yeah, Clint, it's me,' Jeff replied from across the yard. 'What in hell is going on?'

'The Egans are here. But it's OK to come in.' Halloran turned and hurried back into the house.

Buck Egan was stirring. Halloran covered him. Asa Deacon was trying to get to his feet. Boots sounded on the porch and then Jeff came in at the door, holding a pistol. His face was pale. The ride from town had opened his wound and fresh blood stained his shirt.

'I walked into trouble when I got here,' Halloran explained, 'but it's OK now. I don't know where your outfit is. Your pa was on the porch with an empty rifle in his hands and I walked into Buck here, who hit me from behind. There were two Egans, as far as I can make out, but now there is only one.'

'What happened, Pa?' Jeff demanded. He spotted Ham on the couch and crossed to him, dropping to one knee to examine him. 'The doc is on his way here with a posse. He'll be able to fix Ham. So what happened here, huh?'

Asa had given up trying to rise. His mouth was opening and closing but no sounds came from him. Cora came in at the door and hurried across the big room to her mother and Tilda. Halloran watched Buck Egan, who was recovering his senses.

'On your feet, Egan,' Halloran said. 'Sit in that far corner and don't give me any trouble.'

Buck scrambled to his feet. He

moved to the corner Halloran had indicated and flopped down again to hold his head in his hands.

'Get some rope and hogtie him, Jeff,' Halloran said. 'Then I'll take a look around outside. It is almost sunup so we'd better be ready for more trouble.'

Jeff bound Buck Egan's hands and feet and Halloran went out to the porch. The sun was just below the eastern skyline and crimson shafts of sunlight were streaking the grey sky. He drew a deep breath of the cool morning air and released it in a long sigh. He did not like the way this trouble had evolved, much preferring a stand-up fight that would end the shooting quickly. But it had not been his trouble, and the Egans had ruled the course of its development until now.

Halloran made a round of the spread, he found the cook dead in his shack and two of the outfit were also dead near the corral, but there was no sign of Mitchell or anyone else. The signs were that Buck and Ezra Egan had sneaked into the ranch and murdered the Big D men in cold blood. The sun peeped over the horizon as Halloran made his way back to the ranch house. He paused on the porch to examine Ezra Egan, who was dead, and as he turned to enter the house he caught the faint sound of approaching riders.

'Jeff,' he yelled. 'There are riders coming. Get ready in case they are the Egan outfit.'

The door of the house was jerked open and Jeff appeared; gun in hand. Halloran grinned. This was more like it. If the Egans were on the warpath then this trouble could be over before breakfast . . .

10

Halloran and Jeff stood shoulder to shoulder on the porch as the rising sun cast long shadows across the yard. The incoming riders appeared from low ground and took shape in the strengthening daylight.

'Two of them,' Jeff observed.

'Three,' Halloran corrected as another rider appeared. 'Can you make out who they are?'

'Not yet. We'd better be ready for them in case they are not friendly.' Jeff drew his pistol and checked it, and Halloran did likewise.

'It looks like a good day to end a war,' Halloran said.

'Any day would be a good day to stop the trouble we've got,' Jeff replied. 'Say, that's Doc Woollard in the lead, or I'm a monkey's uncle, and that's Jack Hayman and Frank Simmons with him

— two men who turn out regularly with the posse.'

The three riders entered the yard and came across to the house. Jeff stepped down off the porch and he patted the nose of the doc's horse as Woollard dismounted.

'It is good to see you, Doc,' Jeff greeted. 'Pa ain't as bad as Cora thought, but Ham is in a bad way.'

'I'll take a look at them.' Woollard untied his medical bag from his cantle and stepped up on to the porch. He paused to look around. 'Jack, Frank, keep a sharp watch for trouble. I don't trust the Egans.' He glanced at Jeff as he turned to the door of the ranch house. 'We passed Burt Egan and a couple of hard cases on the trail at the point where you ride on to Bar E grass. They didn't interfere with us, but sure looked like they wanted to. Burt had been shot and was covered in blood, but he refused to let me look at him.'

'I winged him earlier,' Halloran said.

'Pity you didn't kill him,' Jeff

observed sourly.

'I hope Cora will get some breakfast going now,' Woollard remarked. 'We'll fight better on full stomachs.'

Jeff nodded. 'The women are busy cooking right now. I'll stay out here and keep watch while you go inside the house, Clint. You can relieve me after you've eaten.'

Halloran watched the two posse men dismount. One of them led their horses over to the corral and the other stepped up on to the porch to chat with Jeff. Halloran went into the house. Doc Woollard was already attending to Ham, who was conscious now but seemed to be in a bad way. Buck Egan was hogtied in a corner, motionless and watchful, looking like a trapped mountain lion, his eyes filled with an angry glare. Asa Deacon was drowsing in a chair in a corner, his rifle by his side. Tilda was seated at the table, reading a book and looking as if she would feel better lying in bed. Cora and Mrs Deacon were busy at the stove. The smell of cooking bacon was already enhancing the atmosphere; Halloran moistened his lips as the smell reawakened his dormant hunger.

'Ham will survive,' Woollard said after a cursory examination of the wounded man. 'He'll be off work for some weeks, but he'll pull through OK.'

Halloran sat down at the table. Tilda looked up at him with troubled eyes. She was in pain from her wound, and Halloran could tell she had emotional problems niggling in her mind.

'I spoke to Mack Egan in town,' he said quietly. 'Do you know he's had no part in this trouble between the Deacons and the Egans? He was going to ride out to talk to his father about calling off the trouble. He said he would come on here afterwards and offer to use his gun against his own family if they did not get off the war path.'

'Talk is cheap,' Tilda replied harshly, 'and he's always talked a lot, but he's never done anything to back up his

232

words. He doesn't care enough about me to stand up to his family.' Tears came to her eyes. 'There's been too much trouble for us to bridge and make a future together. Look at my family. Pa has been shot, Ham is like to die, Jeff is covered in blood, and I'm in pain with a bullet wound. There's hardly anyone in the Deacon and the Egan family that hasn't been shot over the past few days, and it is not over yet, not by a long rope.'

She returned her attention to the book she was reading, and Halloran shook his head. He was silent until Cora came to him with a plate of food. He thanked her quietly and began to eat. He was impatient for the action to start, and could sense a build-up of tension in the atmosphere. He could hear Jeff's voice on the porch as he conversed with the two posse men — their subject of conversation was the trouble. Their whole world consisted of trouble, and Halloran knew they had to put a stop to it as soon as possible.

After he had eaten, Halloran relieved Jeff on the porch, and the two posse men went into the house to have breakfast. Halloran stood at a corner of the porch and watched his surroundings. Nothing moved out on the range, but he sensed that it was too quiet. He fully expected the Egans and their outfit to come helling into the yard with all guns blazing. But when he did see a movement beyond the yard he was surprised at the sight of a single rider who cantered into view and approached the ranch.

It was Mack Egan; the youngster dismounted at the gate and walked his horse across the hardpan to the porch. Halloran watched him intently. He admired Mack's nerve, for he had no friends here.

'I tried to talk my pa out of riding over here with the rest of the outfit,' Mack said when he confronted Halloran, 'but it was no dice. He's intent on wiping out the Deacons, so here I am to stand with you against my family.'

'There's been trouble here already.' Halloran explained how he had ridden in and found Buck and Ezra Egan on the ranch. He indicated the motionless figure lying on the porch to his right, and saw Mack freeze in shock.

When Mack saw the body of his brother Ezra on the porch his expression changed slowly. He shook his head in disbelief.

'I told Pa this was how it would end,' he said in a low tone. 'Where's Buck?'

'He's still alive.' Halloran grimaced. 'I've got him hogtied — he'd grab a gun and start shooting if I turned him loose.'

'Maybe I can talk some sense into him.'

Halloran nodded. 'You can try, but I don't think we can take any chances right now. Hold on and I'll tell Jeff you're here. I don't know what kind of a reception you'll get.'

'I'll risk it,' Mack responded.

Halloran went to the door and opened it. He peered inside the big room and saw Jeff seated at the table.

'We've got a visitor,' Halloran called. 'It's Mack Egan.'

Jeff cursed and got to his feet so fast he overturned his chair, and then he paused and doubled over because pain was darting through his wounded side. He came staggering towards Halloran, his face expressing agony.

'What the hell does he want, Clint?' Jeff demanded. He drew his pistol and cocked it.

Halloran reached out and took the weapon away from Jeff.

'You don't need that, pard,' he said easily. 'Mack is here on a peace mission. He's tried to talk his father into calling off the trouble.'

'I can guess Frank's reaction,' Jeff said stiffly. He looked into Halloran's eyes and relaxed slowly. 'OK,' he said with a sigh. 'I'll hear what he's got to say. I know he's never taken part in the trouble against us. He's probably a good Egan, if there is such a thing.'

Halloran stepped aside and Jeff

walked out on to the porch. He stepped over Ezra Egan's inert body and walked to the edge of the porch to look down at Mack.

'So what's new, Mack?' Jeff asked.

'I wish I could tell you that the trouble has been called off,' Mack replied, with a shake of his head, 'but I can't. I spoke to my father but couldn't get through to him. He's gonna show up here any time now with every gun he can call on. I hope you're ready to stand him off.'

'We'll manage.' Jeff nodded. 'Thanks for the warning, but we've been expecting it. You'd better ride out while you still can. If Frank catches you here you'll be in as much trouble as us.'

'I'm worried about Tilda,' Mack said. 'How is she?'

'She'll live.' Jeff narrowed his eyes as he regarded Mack's face. He saw real concern in the youthful countenance. 'Do you wanta see her before you ride?'

'I'd sure like to. I'll stand with you and fight my father if you'll let me. I told him I was coming over here to talk to you.'

Jeff shook his head. 'I couldn't take a chance on you when the slugs start flying,' he said firmly. 'I'd have to keep an eye on you when I should be concentrating on shooting. Come in and see Tilda, and then leave us to it.'

Mack trailed his reins and followed Jeff into the house. Halloran remained on the porch, looking around. He was holding Jeff's pistol in his right hand. Jeff stood just inside the doorway while Mack walked across the room to where Tilda was seated beside the doctor, who was eating his breakfast. The two posse men were also sitting at the table. Cora was talking to her sister, but fell silent when Mack appeared. Tilda gazed impassively at the man she loved. Her face was pale, her expression resolute, but her eyes showed hopelessness.

'You shouldn't have come here, Mack,' she said. 'I thought you had more sense than the rest of your family.'

'I couldn't keep away.' He lifted his

arms and then let them fall hopelessly. 'I want to be with you, Tilda. I've chosen my side, and I'll stay here if I can.'

'You dirty renegade!' Buck Egan shouted from the corner where he was lying. 'You're chicken-livered! Just wait until I get out of here. I'll take a gun to you myself. You should be out there now with Pa and the rest of them, not mooning around here like a love-sick calf. I hope Pa kills you when he rides in.'

'You've always been a fool, Buck, and you still can't see any further than the end of your nose,' Mack retorted. 'You and Ezra just had to go along with Pa and Uncle Burt, and it was pure greed that set them on this trail. Do you know Ezra is lying dead out on the porch? He sure asked for it, and got it. None of you could see that no matter what you did you just couldn't win. The doctor is here with two men from town, and they can see which way the wind is blowing.'

'Ramsey is the sheriff now Kett is

dead,' Buck reminded, 'and he's always been for us.'

'Ramsey is in jail for killing the sheriff,' Doc Woollard said sharply. 'He's finished around here, and we'll hang him after he's had a trial. There's a big clean-up going on, and that's why we are here now. If Frank rides in looking for trouble he'll get more than he bargains for, and if he lives he'll see the inside of the jail in Plainsville. There'll be no more shilly-shallying as far as the law is concerned. We'll come down hard on anyone disturbing the peace.'

Halloran was watching the approaches to the ranch, and, when he spotted two riders on a crest several hundred yards out, he pushed open the door of the house and looked into the big room.

'Two riders coming,' he reported.

Jeff turned to him and they stood in the doorway looking out across the yard.

'Say, one of them looks like Ramsey,' Jeff observed.

'It is him,' Halloran confirmed. 'Now

240

how did he get out of jail?'

'And that looks like Chris Egan with him.' Jeff used his Stetson to shade his eyes. 'Yeah, it's Chris all right. What in hell are they doing out here?'

'If they keep riding in like they are doing we'll be able to ask them in a few minutes,' Halloran said. 'I'm wondering if they've come straight from town. I would have thought Chris would go to the Egan place before showing up here.'

'Let's get under cover,' Jeff suggested. 'They might ride right into the yard, and we'll be able to get the drop on them.'

They entered the house and closed the door. Jeff went to a window beside the door and peered out. Halloran stood at Jeff's shoulder and they watched the two riders drawing closer. Ramsey reined in at the gate and sat motionless in his saddle observing the ranch.

'They are both armed.' Halloran noted.

'Doc will want them alive,' Jeff responded.

'We need to see if they are alone

241

before we make a move.' Halloran checked his pistol. He glanced at Doc Woollard, who was finishing his breakfast. 'Can you spare a moment, Doc?'

Woollard got up from the table and came across to the window.

Jeff jerked a thumb at the yard. 'Look who has turned up,' he invited.

The doctor peered through the window and uttered an imprecation when he saw the riders.

'That's exactly what I said,' Halloran observed. 'Cover me from here and I'll go out on the porch. They should react to the sight of me and I know how to deal with them.'

'We should go out together,' Jeff said, 'and one of us should have a rifle.'

He glanced around the room, saw the Winchester leaning against the wall beside Asa, and crossed to pick up the weapon. When he found it empty he jerked open a drawer in a dresser and took out a box of shells. His hands shook as he refilled the magazine. Halloran did not take his eyes off the two men out by the gate who were subjecting the ranch to an intent scrutiny. Jeff came back to Halloran's side.

'I'm ready,' he said. 'Let's go and ask them what they want.'

Halloran smiled and opened the door. 'You stay inside, Doc,' he said, and went out to the porch with Jeff close behind him.

Ramsey jerked his pistol from its holster when he saw the door open. Halloran caught the movement and reached for his gun in a fast draw. Chris Egan reined his horse to his left as he pulled a gun. Jeff and Halloran separated on the porch. Halloran fired first. His pistol snaked upwards from his hip and he threw down on Ramsey, squeezing his trigger as the foresight of the pistol covered Ramsey's chest. Ramsey jerked in his saddle when the half inch chunk of lead smacked into him. His gun muzzle, in the act of lifting quickly, suddenly became too heavy for his hand and fell away. His trigger finger jerked convulsively as he died, sending his shot into the dust beside his nervous horse.

When Ramsey fell out of his saddle, Chris Egan swung his horse to ride for cover, twisting in leather to bring his pistol to bear. Gun smoke flared when he triggered the weapon, and slugs crackled across the yard to thud into the front of the house. Jeff lifted the Winchester to his shoulder but found he could not fire it because his left arm was practically useless. He lowered the long gun and thrust it at Halloran.

'Bring him down, Clint,' Jeff said urgently.

Halloran took the rifle and aimed it at Chris Egan galloping for cover. Egan's pistol was swinging as he continued to try and bring it to bear on the porch. Halloran fired. The weapon cracked and smoked. Egan threw his arms wide and arched his back as the rifle slug struck him. His pistol flew from his hand and he slumped forward over the neck of his horse. Before

Halloran could fire again, horse and rider had disappeared over a crest. Echoes growled sullenly across the range.

The door of the house was jerked open and Doc Woollard appeared on the porch, grasping his medical bag.

'You're wasting your time, Doc,' Halloran observed as the doctor set off across the yard. 'You should have brought an undertaker with you.'

Woollard kept going at a half run. He reached Ramsey's side and bent over the prostrate man. But at that moment he heard the sound of approaching hoofs and looked up at the crest where Chris Egan had disappeared. His eyes narrowed when he saw a group of riders coming into view.

'Doc, get back here!' Halloran called urgently. 'The Egans are coming!'

Woollard took a step towards the house but changed his mind and dropped to one knee beside Ramsey only to discover that the crooked ex-deputy was dead. Woollard shook his head and picked up his bag. He turned and walked back towards the house with methodical steps, refusing to look over his shoulder when the dozen riders, with Frank Egan leading them, came galloping off the crest to make a bee line for the house, their hoofs thundering on the hard ground.

'Run, Doc,' Halloran called, levering a fresh shell into the breech of the rifle.

Frank Egan raised his pistol and aimed at the doctor. When he fired, Woollard broke his stride and fell forward on to his face. Halloran swung the rifle, lined it up on Frank Egan, and squeezed the trigger. Frank dropped his pistol as the 44.40 slug tore through his left shoulder. But he kept coming, and snatched a rifle out of his saddle scabbard. Halloran turned to run for the cover of the house; Jeff beat him inside, and slammed the door when Halloran joined him.

'They shot Doc,' Jeff shouted.

The two posse men came running towards the door, reaching for their guns. Halloran raised a hand to stop them going out to the porch. Before he could speak a volley of shots rang out and a swarm of slugs tore into the woodwork of the house. Halloran saw one of the posse men stagger. He reached out and grasped Jeff, pushed him to the ground, and followed him down as more lead came blasting into the weathered woodwork. Slugs shattered the front windows and crackled across the room. Tilda slid off her seat and crouched cowering on the floor; Cora grabbed her mother and pushed her down to safety against the front wall. She produced a pistol and crouched at a nearby window, ready to fight. Mack Egan stood for a moment, shocked by the action. A slug tore a gash in his left forearm and blood spurted. He threw himself down and crawled to Halloran's side.

'How many are there?' Mack demanded.

'About ten,' Halloran replied. 'Keep your head down or they'll blow it off. Wait until their shooting dwindles, then give it to them if you've a mind to fight

247

against your own side.'

'They are not on my side,' Mack replied.

The shooting did not lessen; slugs crackled into the front of the house like storm rain. Halloran tried to look outside but bullets whined and thumped around him and he ducked. He could hear hot lead smacking into cooking utensils on the stove, making the pots jump and ring in high pitched notes of metallic fury. He looked around the big room; dust was flying and early morning sunlight beamed through the bullet holes that had opened up in the woodwork.

By degrees the shooting diminished. Halloran tried again to peer outside, and managed to get a sight of what was happening across the yard. The riders had dismounted and gained cover from which to shoot. Gun smoke was drifting in an acrid cloud across the yard. Halloran thrust his pistol over the windowsill and triggered three quick shots at heads and faces peering towards the house. Men ducked and the shooting lessened immediately. Jeff sprang up and emptied his Colt at the attackers. Then the shooting faded until an uneasy silence settled over the ranch.

'Jeff, I'll go out the back way and attack them from a corner of the house,' Halloran called, and slid away across the room to make for the kitchen.

He opened the back door cautiously and peered out. The shooting out front started up again. He paused to reload his pistol; he left the house and ran along the back to the right and then down the side of the house to a front corner. He saw two attackers on the move to approach the rear of the house and waited for them to draw closer. They spotted him and opened fire. Halloran heard the thud of lead striking the wall around him. A splinter of wood slashed across his left cheek and he felt blood running down his chin. He fired two quick shots and both men went down heavily: did not move again.

Halloran showed his teeth in a

mirthless grin. This was more like it. He peered around the corner and looked across the yard. Frank Egan was on his feet waving a pistol and exhorting his outfit to rush the house. Fire was being directed at Frank from inside the house, but he appeared to have a charmed life. Halloran aimed at him, triggered his pistol, and the rancher jerked and pitched sideways into the dust. Those of his men who had arisen to attack the house hastily changed their minds when Frank went down, and Halloran picked his targets and fired, taking men out with each shot.

The shooting at the house ceased abruptly. Halloran, peering around the corner, saw some of the attackers withdrawing, and increased his rate of fire. A skilled gunman, he rarely missed with a shot, and his accuracy knocked out targets with deadly regularity. He moved around the corner and stood with his back against the front wall of the house, ready to trade shots with any who wished to take him on. He grinned when he saw the survivors of the Egan crew running to their horses, and hurried them on their way with questing shots that took a further toll of their numbers.

Gun echoes were growling sullenly in the distance as if reluctant to quit the scene. Halloran walked across the yard, gun in hand, to check Frank Egan. He found the rancher dead, his upturned face set in a mask of hatred and defiance. The door of the house was opened and Jeff came out to the porch. They both converged on the prostrate doctor, and Halloran was relieved to find Woollard alive and conscious. He had a blood stain on the back of his coat high on the left shoulder.

'I feared you were dead, Doc,' Halloran observed.

'When Frank Egan shot me I thought it would be safer to stay down until the shooting ended,' Woollard replied.

'Frank Egan should have done the same,' Halloran said. 'He's lying dead behind you, Doc. Come on, let us get you into the house.'

Jeff helped the doctor to his feet and pushed a shoulder into Woollard's left armpit. They crossed the porch and Halloran opened the door for them. He paused to glance around the yard as they entered the house. There were several bodies lying in the dust — none of them moving. The sun was now well clear of the horizon and the breeze blowing across the range was beginning to heat up.

Halloran went into the house to find Woollard slumped to the floor and Jeff standing with his hands shoulder high. Mack Egan was beside Tilda, and he was talking fast to Buck Egan, who was standing in the corner where he had been bound. But now he was free of his bonds, and had Asa Deacon up out of his chair. He was holding the old man with his left hand and covering everyone in the room with the pistol he had snatched from Asa's holster.

'You thought you had me, huh?' Buck snarled.

'Don't be a fool, Buck, put that gun down,' Mack rapped. 'Pa is lying dead out in the yard because he couldn't listen to reason and Ezra is down on the porch. Now you're itching to go the same way. Why don't you get some sense into your thick head and give up?'

'I'm gonna shoot every last one of you, including you, Mack,' Buck blustered. 'You're a turncoat, and you're gonna be the first to get it.'

'Can't you see it's all over?' Mack demanded. 'The Deacons have won. There's only you and me to run Bar E now. Bury the hatchet and we'll get on with our lives.'

'No dice!' Buck snarled.

Halloran was covered from Buck's view by Jeff. He stepped half a pace to his right and palmed his pistol. The weapon came out of its holster fast and smoothly: Halloran cocked it. Buck heard the sound and swung his hand to cover Halloran. He thrust Asa aside as his muzzle sought Halloran like a wolf sniffing out prey. Mack set his right hand into action. He made a fast draw, his gun rasping out of its holster. Buck paused and then turned his gun back to his brother. Halloran did not hesitate. He raised his gun and fired twice. His slugs smacked into Buck's chest and flung him backwards against the wall.

Buck lost his grip on his gun and it fell from his fingers. He leaned back against the wall, his face showing surprise. Then his legs lost their strength and he slid down the wall into a sitting position, his chin down on his chest.

Mack Egan glanced at Halloran, his expression showing thanks because he had not been compelled to shoot his brother. The echoes died away to nothing, and Halloran hoped that would be the last of the shooting. He reloaded his gun before holstering it, and then went forward to help Mrs Deacon to her feet. It was time to let the dust settle. Later would be time enough to pick up the pieces . . .

We do hope that you have enjoyed reading this large print book.

Did you know that all of our titles are available for purchase?

We publish a wide range of high quality large print books including:
Romances, Mysteries, Classics
General Fiction
Non Fiction and Westerns

Special interest titles available in large print are:
The Little Oxford Dictionary
Music Book, Song Book
Hymn Book, Service Book

Also available from us courtesy of Oxford University Press:
Young Readers' Dictionary
(large print edition)
Young Readers' Thesaurus
(large print edition)

For further information or a free brochure, please contact us at:
Ulverscroft Large Print Books Ltd.,
The Green, Bradgate Road, Anstey,
Leicester, LE7 7FU, England.
Tel: (00 44) **0116 236 4325**
Fax: (00 44) **0116 234 0205**

Other titles in the
Linford Western Library:

HOMBRE'S VENGEANCE

Toots J. Johnson

After witnessing his father's murder at the hands of cattle baron Dale Bryant, fifteen-year-old Zachariah Smith grows up fast. Struggling alone to survive fully occupies his mind — until he meets two of Bryant's other victims. He realises that he must join the fight for justice and avenge his father's death, knowing that lead will fly and he will probably die trying to stop Bryant. But now Zac is a man, and it is time for the hombre's vengeance!

IRON EYES IS DEAD

Rory Black

Desert Springs was an oasis that drew the dregs of Texas down into its profitable boundaries. Among the many ruthless characters, there was none so fearsome as the infamous bounty hunter, Iron Eyes. He had trailed a dangerous outlaw right into the remote settlement. But Iron Eyes was wounded: shot up with arrow and bullet after battling with a band of Apaches. As the doctor fought to save him, was the call true that Iron Eyes was dead?

TAKE THE OREGON TRAIL

Eugene Clifton

Thousands of men had taken the trail to the west looking for a new beginning — many didn't make it. Adam Trant had also set out on the Oregon Trail — but he was looking for an old enemy. The hunt took him to a savage wilderness and matched him against deadly marauders. Adam was ready to die, as long as he succeeded in his quest. However, he wasn't ready for the unpredictable force of the love of a woman.